Colleen Rowan Kosinski

A PROMISE
STITCHED
IN TIME

Designed by Danielle D. Farmer
Cover Design by Brenda McCallum
Cover art by Colleen Rowan Kosinski

Type set in Mailart Rubberstamp/Fenice/Archer/Goudy Old Style

ISBN: 978-0-7643-5554-7
Printed in China

Published by Schiffer Publishing, Ltd.
4880 Lower Valley Road
Atglen, PA 19310
Phone: (610) 593-1777; Fax: (610) 593-2002
E-mail: Info@schifferbooks.com
Web: www.schifferbooks.com

For our complete selection of fine books on this and related subjects, please visit our website at www.schifferbooks.com. You may also write for a free catalog.

Schiffer Publishing's titles are available at special discounts for bulk purchases for sales promotions or premiums. Special editions, including personalized covers, corporate imprints, and excerpts, can be created in large quantities for special needs. For more information, contact the publisher.

We are always looking for people to write books on new and related subjects. If you have an idea for a book, please contact us at proposals@schifferbooks.com.

OTHER SCHIFFER BOOKS FOR MIDDLE-GRADE READERS:

Just One Thing!, Nancy Viau, 978-0-7643-5162-4
Beauty and Bernice, Nancy Viau, 978-0-7643-5580-6
Captive, Donna Stoltzfus, 978-0-7643-5551-6

A Promise Stitched in Time was originally inspired by a true story of two women held prisoner at Auschwitz who were forced, under severe conditions, to make luxury garments for Commandant Hoess's family. The identities of these prisoners have never been discovered.

CHAPTER ONE

Nine days, nineteen hours until the deadline.

I gaze up through bare trees as my bike bumps along the worn woodland path and wonder what color the sky is today. Some might consider it cerulean or maybe even ultramarine blue. Dad would've known the color right away, but I still have to think about it.

Lately, I've been examining everything around me, pondering its color composition in preparation for my scholarship entry to the Peabody Summer Arts Academy in Princeton, New Jersey. I've mixed a gazillion color palettes in my mind, but I still can't find an inspiration for my art piece. And I only have nine days and nineteen hours left to complete it.

Just when I think I've nailed the paint colors for the sky, my bike jolts and I go flying. Landing with a hard thud, the air whooshes from my lungs and I feel a moment of déjà vu. Needlelike objects poke my skin. Flat on my back in a cluster of brambles, I turn my head and see the twisted tree root.

I am about as graceful as Bambi on ice. Examining my injuries, I notice tiny scratches criss-crossing the skin on my hands, already becoming angry red bumps. I run my fingertips over the abrasions and study them. Carnelian red. Kind of pretty, if they didn't sting so badly.

I tug loose the last of the twigs entwined with strands of my hair. Maybe a bird will find them in the spring and weave a bit of my DNA into its nest.

One particularly puffy cloud moves across the horizon. It reminds me of Dad's billowing mass of hair. I'd promised him I'd get into Peabody and I am determined to keep that promise. I brush myself off and get back on my bike.

Shades of blue still spinning in my head, I skid to a stop in front of the Salvation Army Thrift Store, hoping to find an object of inspiration. I peer through the window on tiptoes. My breath mists the glass, so I wipe it clear with my coat sleeve. Sometimes the front window display holds really unique or funky objects, fun things to paint like dolls with bristles for hair and marble eyes that follow you wherever you go, lamps dripping with way too many crystals, or wax fruit complete with bite marks from indiscriminate diners.

But not this day. Through the smudged glass I spot the manager, Mrs. Biggs, placing a china teapot on a shelf in the back. *Now, that has possibilities.*

As I open the door, musty air and the scent of mothballs and lemon floor cleaner hit my nose. When I pull off my wool hat, my hair crackles with electricity and sticks to my neck and cheeks. With a lick of my palms I smooth it down before making a beeline down the aisle.

A boy who looks about my age ambles around a table of books. The golden-brown hue of his skin triggers imaginary colors swirling about in my mind's eye. How would I paint his complexion in oils? Too much yellow would make his skin tone sallow. Maybe a rich honey-brown, somewhere between ochre and sienna. That would do the trick.

My gaze travels up to his face. The boy's deep-set eyes and long lashes give him a dreamy expression. Puppy dog eyes.

Too bad he's ruined his look with a seriously nerdy newsboy cap. My sister Patty would click her tongue and call it a major fashion no-no. Locks of hair even darker than his eyes tumble out from under the bill of the cap and fall across his brow. Best not to stare too long. I have to finish my painting. No time for boys.

Just one last look at his eyes and, oh no, he's caught me.

I turn my head and concentrate on the china teapot Mrs. Biggs placed on the shelf. Age has crackled the delicate porcelain so that the dainty violets twining over the cream china resemble a mosaic. It might make a beautiful painting if I could get the details right.

Boots knock on the linoleum behind me. "Maggie McConnell?"

I swing around and push back my hair, eyebrows raised. "Um, yeah?"

He smiles and my cheeks get hot. I peek at myself in a silver mirror next to the teapot. The freckles generously sprinkled across my face look like cinnamon-colored stars in a magenta sky.

"You don't remember, do you?"

I shift from foot to foot, thinking.

"Preschool. You and I hung out in the art activity corner constantly."

Images of fingerpaints, newsprint, and craft glue run through my mind, a collage that leads me to, "Taj?"

"You do remember me." He sticks his hands in his pockets. "It's been a long time."

I remember him clearly now. His big, brown eyes and lopsided smile. We'd been inseparable. The dynamic art duo, they'd called us. The teachers constantly tried to get us to participate in other activities, but we always snuck back to the art station as quickly as we could. "How are you?" I ask. "You moved during the middle of kindergarten, right?"

"Albuquerque, New Mexico. I—"

The brass bells hanging on the front door jingle. I turn and my stomach drops. In walks the woman from the local antique shop, *The Treasure Chest*. She has a head full of frizzy curls, and secretly I've always called her Poodlehead—a stuck-up, yippy little mutt. I know this is mean—she can't help how her hair looks, but I can't keep the poodles from prancing around in my head every time I see her. Then I notice Poodlehead's eyes zeroing in on the teapot. I grab the bone-china handle, claiming it for myself.

"If you see anything good, grab it fast or she'll take it," I say to Taj. I flick my gaze back to Poodlehead and his eyes follow.

I move along the shelves with the teapot clutched to my chest. The squeaky wheels of Poodlehead's cart gain momentum. Taj follows me, then pauses to examine a novel.

He snatches up a copy of *A Wrinkle in Time* and gives me a thumbs up.

When he turns back to the shelves, my eyes move quickly up and down his body. Brass-buckled shoes, suspenders, and that hat. The way he dresses makes him look like he could have been transported here from another place or time. Reminds me of an episode of *Dr. Who*. I glance around, looking for a dark-blue phone booth masking the Tardis.

Poodlehead's breath blows hot on the back of my neck when I spy a golden water goblet. It might make a cool painting if I could capture the way its shiny surface mirrors the objects around it. I decide I need it. But then Poodlehead's hand reaches over my arm and her fingers stretch toward my find!

"Not this time, kid," she spits out.

My eyes meet hers. "Oh, yeah?" I grab it. Juggling the teapot and the goblet, I try to hold onto both of them, but the goblet slips from my hand. Falling, falling, Taj and I try to catch it, and in the process clunk skulls. Before it hits the floor, he catches it.

"Sorry," I mumble, rubbing my head.

"You always were the clumsy one." He nudges my arm.

I try my best to look indignant but can't help laughing. "Some things never change."

"Not always a bad thing. In fact, some things get better." He holds the goblet out toward me.

I giggle like I am in preschool again.

Poodlehead moves farther down the aisle, shooting dirty looks our way. I wish I had magic powers and could zap her into another place and time.

As I take the goblet from Taj, my gaze skips over his shoulder, and I see it—the object that could win me the scholarship. I don't exactly know why, it's just a coat, but deep in my gut I know I must have it. The dime-sized birthmark under the left side of my collarbone tingles and my head buzzes with excitement. "I changed my mind. She can have them." I shove the goblet and the teapot back on the shelf and head down the aisle.

"Okay, well it was nice seeing you again. Maybe . . ." Taj's voice fades behind me. I am zeroed in. Nothing else exists except that coat.

The gray tweed coat draped over a thread-worn dressmaker's form draws me closer: *Maggie, Maggie*, it chants, practically singing my name.

Its collar is some sort of fur, the real thing—black mink maybe? I can't stop my feet from moving toward it.

My palms stretch, tingling in anticipation, ready to feel its nubby wool tickling my skin. Just as my fingers are about to grab hold, an old lady reeking of baby powder and wintergreen pushes her overflowing cart between it and me. I fly backward into the arms of a male mannequin sporting a hot-pink Speedo. Ick! I twist away.

The old lady gives me the once-over, flashes a yellow-toothed smile, and snatches the coat. "Too mature-looking for you anyway," she huffs, tossing it in her cart.

"Wait, I—"

She rolls toward the next aisle.

Alone by the naked dress form with my hands balled at my sides, I exhale slowly and claim an empty cart, returning to the shelves of glassware to try to forget about the coat. I glance around. Taj is gone.

I can't get the image of the tweed coat out of my head; the thought of losing it makes my scalp prickle. But maybe she's right. I am a thirteen-year-old girl. The coat suits her better anyway.

I meander down the aisles pushing the squeaky-wheeled cart, my mind preoccupied with thoughts of the coat. The herringbone pattern of gray and black weaves through my mind like M. C. Escher's birds in his lithograph *Liberation*, threading in and out in a blur of gray. Its tweed threads spool around me, refusing to loosen their hold.

My hand reaches up to scratch my birthmark. It burns like crazy. My feet move faster and I catch up to the wrinkled old woman who now possesses the coat. My coat. It is thrown haphazardly in her cart along with a puke-green sweater, neon-orange stretch pants, and a glitter-covered burgundy candle shaped like a monkey.

My inspiration has been missing for a very long time—a little less than three years, to be exact—and even though I'm not sure if my desire for the coat is exactly artistic inspiration, it makes me feel *something*, and I need it. Bad.

The woman is now camped out in the corner of the store with her back to me, trying on shoes. Her cart sits unguarded behind her. I dig my hands into her cart and curl my fingers around the coat's scratchy sleeve. With a yank I free it from the pile, then bolt to the checkout.

"Nine-sixty." The cashier snaps her gum and slips the coat into a plastic bag.

I fish a ten out of my pocket, slap it on the counter, and with the bag in my sweaty hand, make my getaway.

"Your change," the cashier calls after me as I sprint out the door.

I jump on my bike and pedal down the empty street, racing home with my prize. At a stop sign, I lift the tweed coat from the bag, drape it across my handlebars, and lovingly touch the nubby fibers, then slide my fingers over the velvety, soft fur around the collar. The thought of animal skins used for decoration normally disgusts me, and I wonder why I am making this exception.

Deep inside I know something is special about this coat. It looks ordinary enough but is totally outdated. The buttons are round, big as quarters, and covered in black velvet. The contrasting textures of slippery fur, soft velvet, and scratchy tweed might make an interesting painting, one that could wow the Peabody Arts Council.

The left lapel has loose threads hanging from it, as if a patch had been sewn on long ago. For some strange reason these threads *really* bother me. I am in the middle of the street but I have to get them out, *now*. Holding the coat closer, my fingers pull at one of the hanging threads.

"Wake up, girl," yells a pointy-nosed man in a car behind me.

I am totally in his way. Despite the chilly March wind, my face goes hot. Still, I *have* to free the thread I am working on. With my fingernail I loosen it and pluck it from the fabric.

He lays on his horn.

"Sorry." I back my bike toward the curb.

He drives by slowly. Out of the corner of my eye I catch his angry stare and try to ignore it. With my head down, I pull the rest of the loose ebony threads from the left lapel. The breeze lifts them away and the coat seems to sigh with relief.

My fingers long to hug the coat close to my body, but in my head I hear my mother's voice telling me to wash it first—*you have no idea where that coat's been.*

I am about to shove it back in the bag, but it calls to me again. It demands I smell it. *Sniff.* Nothing gross, just the ghost of a scent I can't decipher. Despair? It is as if I can actually smell sadness, taste it on the back of my throat. As if the wearer of this coat had not wanted to let it go.

Chapter Two

Nine days, seventeen hours until the deadline.

Home. My eyes skip over our small, bungalow-style house. The front porch sags. In some places the saffron paint peels in curly ribbons, reminding me of lemon rind. The windows and siding droop toward the middle like a house of cards ready to fall in on itself.

The bare maple tree in the side yard still holds the tire swing Dad hung up for my older sister, Patty, and me when we were little. The weathered tire creaks as it sways back and forth in the cold wind. I remember how Patty and I would squish together in the tire like two peas in a pod, holding tight to the rope and giggling while Dad pushed us and chanted, "The owl and the pussycat went to sea in a beautiful pea-green boat. They took some honey and plenty of money wrapped up in a five-pound note."

Exactly three years ago I sat in this same spot on the front lawn with Dad, both at our easels, the scent of turpentine dancing on the breeze. His eyes, the color of clover veiled with morning fog, gleamed with happiness as we enjoyed the unseasonably warm March day.

"Luck of the Irish, my Maggie May," he said.

We painted and talked of plans to open our own art studio one day—never guessing that like acid corroding a lithography plate, a terrible monster was destroying our dream as we spoke. Six months later, cancer stole him. Luck of the Irish? Right.

I frown as I regard the "For Sale" sign that has been stuck in our lawn for the last two months. I pull it out and move it closer to a clump of forsythia bushes. Once

April comes, the branches will fill with bright yellow blossoms and obscure the sign. I clap the dirt off my hands and head inside.

In the kitchen, Patty stands at the stove, stirring a big pot of stew. The smells of celery, onions, and beef surround me as I swing the coat behind my back and try to slink through the kitchen. My fat, spotted cat, Seurat, nearly trips me as he weaves between my legs, purring up a storm. I rescued him last month from under the porch of the nursing home where I volunteer after school. He is eternally grateful—at least that's what I like to think. "Excuse me, Seurat."

Patty sets down the spoon and turns. "You're gonna stick with that dorky name? Sounds like you're calling him Sir Rat. Not very cool for a cat."

Seurat meows. "See, he likes it." I give him an approving smile. Thanks for backing me up, kitty.

"If you say so." Patty shoots me a squinty look as I sidestep through the room. "Hold up. What did you get?" Patty nods toward the big plastic bag peeking out from behind my back.

She'll think my coat purchase is wacky. I tell myself I don't care, just as my left eye starts to twitch.

"Come on, hand it over."

I toss her the bag. "Knock yourself out."

"What is this?" She laughs and slaps her thigh. "Miss Maggie Animals-Have-Rights-Too McConnell bought herself a coat with a fur collar. And you had the nerve to guilt me out of getting the fur-lined boots I wanted to buy last month! I guess you finally came 'round to my way of thinking."

A smug smile tugs at Patty's lips. She loses the grin when she pulls the tweed coat out of the bag and holds it up.

My heart skips a beat when I see the coat in Patty's hands. The coat's scent whispers to me again. There is something comforting, like a warm hug, in the scent. It mingles with the smell of the bubbling stew.

"You don't plan on actually wearing this, do you? It's totally ugful. Are you getting your fashion tips from those old farts you hang out with?"

Those "old farts" are the residents of the Silver Lake Home for Seniors where I volunteer, doing arts and crafts with the residents. Not only does the owner slip me a few bucks every week, but, more importantly, I receive community service points so I can belong to the Honor Society at school. The Honor Society will impress those reading my application for the Peabody Summer Arts Academy Scholarship.

Patty holds the coat at arm's length by her thumb and forefinger. "Anyway, we wear matching coats. You like wearing our matching coats, don't you?"

"No. I mean yes, of course I like our coats." I really hate wearing the matching navy pea coats. They only emphasize the differences between us. And believe me, it's more than just her ten-month age advantage. Even though we are technically in the same grade at school, she can easily pass for sixteen. "I didn't buy it to wear. I'm thinking of painting it for an art contest."

"Thank. God. Wearing that old thing would be a class one what-not-to-wear mistake. How much?"

"Nine-sixty."

"You wasted almost ten bucks? I thought we were saving to go to the movies next week."

"I am," I say, and snatch the coat back. "Something about this coat is special. I can't explain it." I absently stroke the soft fur on the collar. "I'm going to run it up to our room."

"Better hurry, Picasso, Mom will be home in a few minutes."

"I prefer Georgia O'Keeffe to Picasso, if you don't mind." I nudge her lightly with my shoulder. "And please, don't tell Mom." I glance down at the black-and-gray coat draped over my arm. My heart races again.

"Didn't see a thing, okay? Now get your rear in gear. I need help." She goes back to preparing dinner.

I hurry toward the door, pass the kitchen table, and then do a double take. There are only three chairs at the table. "Where's the other chair?"

"Broken. Threw it out."

"You what!" I scream.

"It. Was. Broken." She glares at me.

"It. Is. Dad's." I match her stare.

Patty clunks the spoon into the sink and plants her hands on her hips. "It was, but obviously he doesn't need it anymore." Her face softens. "The leg was screwed up. It was dangerous, Mags."

"We could have fixed it."

"Old people. Old coats. The past, Maggie. It's been three years. You gotta let it go."

"I don't have to do anything," I shout and run upstairs.

I kick the side of Patty's bed before collapsing on my own. Laying the coat across my lap, I pet its fur collar until my breathing steadies. I tuck the tweed coat down into the crevice between my mattress and the heather-green wall and draw my covers over it. I smooth down my blue blanket for extra security. Patty won't be ditching my coat, too.

Seurat pads over, sniffs the hiding spot, and then buries his nose in my blanket as if it is hiding a mound of catnip. Eventually he curls into a ball, tucks his crooked tail around him, and closes his eyes.

Against opposite walls in our room sit twin beds and white painted nightstands holding pink ginger jar lamps with cream-colored shades. Nail polish bottles, perfumes, and hair clips clutter Patty's nightstand. My nightstand holds acorns, blue jay feathers, and my favorite find—a delicately scaled pearly green snakeskin. All of my treasures were collected on the daily hikes Dad and I used to take before he got too sick to walk with me.

Taped to the wall next to my pillow is Georges Seurat's painting *La Grande Jatte*. I ripped it out of an old issue of *American Artist* magazine in honor of the name I chose for my cat. Patty calls it "my lady with the big blue butt." I tried to explain to her that the woman in the painting is wearing a bustle, but every time she says the words, she cracks herself up so much she doesn't hear a thing I say.

After one last glance at the coat's hiding place, I go next door to the tiny room Dad used as a studio. His leather-scented aftershave still lingers in the corners. I touch my hand to his sketches taped to the walls and trace my finger over the fairies, banshees, and other magical creatures he drew.

My dad told me that when he was a little boy, my grandma would gather him up in a red flannel blanket and rock him in her creaky rocker in front of their stone fireplace, telling him stories about the creatures he drew. When he told me the same stories of a mythical place called Tir Na Nog in his deep, lilting voice, I used to imagine myself in front of that comfy, warm hearth. Safe and happy. It was so easy to imagine back then.

I touch a finger to my easel and think back to the time I first asked Dad if I could paint with him. Immediately he set down his brush and made me leave the room, whispering, "I have a surprise for you." I laid on the floor in the hall outside the door and listened to him humming as he rattled about the room.

For the final reveal he held his hands over my eyes, his fingers scented with varnish and soap. When he released his hands I found a new set of paints tied with a red bow next to an easel with my name on it. The corner of a glossy brochure stuck out from under the paint set. Dad slid it out and handed it to me. "See this? The Peabody Arts Academy. Best in the country. I'd love to see my darlin' girl learnin' from the likes of these folks."

I took the brochure and ran my fingers over the smooth paper. The Academy looked like a magical castle. A place where dreams could come true.

"Can I go now, Daddy?" I asked.

"Not until you're thirteen, munchkin. Don't worry, that gives us years to build those skills, my little Miss."

"I'm going to go there one day. I promise."

He wrapped me in one of his big bear hugs, safe and tight. "You'll make me proud," he whispered in my ear.

It seems like only yesterday, but also a hundred years ago. I'll never feel his joy again. Sadness paints my thoughts black.

His easel still holds the painting he did of our house three years ago as we sat side by side on the front lawn. If you look carefully, you can see Mom's face staring out the upstairs window and Patty's shadow by the side of the house. I suck in my breath and turn away. Dad's last painting.

My easel displays the painting of Seurat I keep working and reworking, intending to submit to the Arts Council before the deadline. I've been painting it for weeks but just can't seem to get it right. I planned on using the pointillism technique in honor of my cat's namesake. Georges Seurat created the method of using dots of color to create images. I thought the judges might find it clever and inventive, but this painting is nothing but a big fail.

Thing is, my art teacher, Ms. Cherry, said the winning painting must be something that resonates with the judges. "It must evoke a feeling," she said. Feelings. Emotions. Sometimes I am so flooded with emotions I am paralyzed, as if I am a broken vase glued together with binder that has not yet hardened. Struggling to stand still. The glue still so tacky I risk falling apart with the slightest bump. Other times I am completely empty of emotion. Like the cracks in me have let them spill away, lost forever.

I now have less than ten days to magically make my painting of Seurat inspiring. Breathe emotion into it. I am afraid I may need a fairy godmother to turn this painting into something special.

Back in my bedroom I smooth my covers one last time, and make sure they hide every inch of the tweed coat. I know it should be placed on a hanger in the closet, but a voice deep inside me insists I hide it. I don't know where this voice comes from. A scary thought enters my mind and I shake my head to clear it away.

But I still obey.

In the kitchen I click on the small television on the counter. It doesn't really matter what's on, as long as it fills the silence. I find an old episode of *Star Trek*. Good. Beam me away.

I fold paper napkins and place them next to the forks on the table. Mom bursts in, shedding her marshmallow-woman quilted parka, and bringing in the scent of rich coffee, courtesy of Dunkin' Donuts. Mom probably has more coffee than blood running through her veins. She dumps her work supplies, empty buckets, and portable vacuum cleaner on the floor.

"Dinner smells heavenly, darlin'," she says with just a trace of her Irish accent. "Sorry I'm a wee bit late again. You got my text?"

"No problem, Mom," Patty says. Patty and I have to share a cell phone, but usually Patty has it. Doesn't matter. Nobody calls me anyway.

Mom takes the wooden spoon from Patty's hand, gives the stew a swirl and a quick taste. "Maggie." Her eyes sweep the table, then roll. "Do you expect us to butter our bread with our fingers, love?" She changes the television channel to a soap opera. Mom hates science fiction.

"Sorry, forgot the butter knives. I'll get them." I rummage through the silverware drawer. "Um, did you notice Dad's chair is missing?"

Patty turns and glowers at me. Mom sinks into her chair and cracks her neck. The lines around her eyes have deepened over the last couple of months, and her hands look raw and stiff as she flexes them. "What?"

I gather the butter knives in my hand. "Patty threw it away."

"It was broken, Mom. She's being a big baby." She hisses under her breath at me, "Way to throw me under the bus, brat."

"I just think she should have asked you first, Mom. You might have wanted to fix—"

"It's fine. We don't need to hold onto broken things."

Her words hit me like a slap in the face.

Patty flops in her chair. "Told you so."

Dishes done, I bound up the steps to take a big whiff of the coat before Patty joins me in our room. The scent is something I can't explain, something teetering on the tip of my senses like a finger, beckoning me forward. I want to follow that crooked finger, but another part of me shouts a warning, pulling me back, as if following would lead me across a tightrope suspended over unknown terrors.

I shake my head and blink my eyes. This is silly, but I still breathe it in and relax the way I used to when I inhaled the fresh balsam-scented forest during morning walks with Dad.

I peek down the hallway to make sure I am completely alone upstairs, and then bring the tweed coat into Dad's studio, shut the door, and try it on. Its tawny satin lining slides smoothly against my skin and its soft fur lightly brushes my neck with a slight tickle. It warms me to the core.

My muscles loosen, and every inch of me melts as I sink toward the floor. I close my eyes, enveloped in darkness. My body bends until I am crouched on the floor, rocking back and forth on my heels like a buoy, my arms wrapped around me and my eyes closed. I find myself humming an odd tune, adrift in a strange sea. Seurat knocks over a cup of brushes, sending them clattering to the floor, and the trance is broken. *What was that song I was humming?*

Seurat rubs against me, purring, and I blink back tears. For once I'm not thinking about Dad. I don't know why I'm crying. I swipe the tears away.

Downstairs the television clicks off, so I quickly shed the coat and set it up to paint. Its absence from my skin leaves me with a chill, as if a frost has settled over my bones.

I turn on the radio and get ready to work.

In the cupboard above a small sink Dad keeps a collection of rags to use for painting. I grab a handful and dislodge a photo stuck in the corner of the shelf. It floats to the floor and lands face up. I stare back at my aunt, my mom's sister Bridget. I have a vague recollection of Dad planning on painting Bridget's portrait as a surprise for Mom. But in the early stages of the painting Mom caught wind of the project and made him stop. Just the mention of Bridget's name makes her eyes red and teary.

Bridget was a musician—a harpist. Quite famous, from the stories Dad told about her. But, like lots of creative people, she had some powerful demons whispering in her ear. Her world started disintegrating by the time she reached the age of twenty-four, and she was hospitalized for schizophrenia. By twenty-five, she orchestrated her final curtain call. Massive overdose. I return her photograph to the cupboard and face my painting.

With only one canvas, I decide to paint over my cat and concentrate on the coat. In long, bold strokes I cover the entire canvas with black, and then weave in snatches of white and gray. Switching to an extra-fine brush, I narrow my eyes and delicately crosshatch portions of the painting. With a fan brush I manipulate the paint to capture the appearance of fur.

As I paint, I think about the chance meeting with my preschool friend, Taj. We had some good times together when we were small. One time we dared each other to taste the fingerpaints to see if the colors tasted differently from each other. I was sure the red would taste like cherry pie. It didn't. Then when we got caught, we swore we didn't do it, even though we had a rainbow of colors smeared on our mouths. I hope I'll run into him again so I can apologize for abandoning him today.

I paint for hours. Finally I sit back and wipe the sweat from my brow, ready to examine my painting with a critical eye.

A huge, splotchy mess faces me. It looks more like a tar roof splattered with pigeon poop than a tweed coat. So much for my new-found inspiration. I throw my brush at the painting, and it slips through the slick paint before hitting the floor.

Exhausted, I drag myself, along with the coat, to my bed and close my eyes. Thoughts of the coat swirl in tiny eddies of my mind. A curtain of fog falls over me.

The gray mist clears and I find myself snuggled up in the tweed coat. Warmth and peace surround me. It is nice, as if nothing in the world can go wrong.

Then my world tips like the bucket seat of a Ferris wheel. The girl in my dream isn't me. There is another face. A foreign face. She wears my tweed coat. Her mouth is open and I can see her lips move, but the only sound I hear is the howl of the wind.

Dark branches like bony fingers claw at the sky behind this brown-eyed girl. She looks wild as she shivers in the tweed coat. A sky-blue ribbon flutters away in the wind whirling about her. Her hand reaches out to retrieve the tie, but it floats out of her grasp. Tiny twigs and leaves tangle in the mess of her dark brown tresses, and there is something, some kind of patch, on the coat's left lapel, but I can't see it clearly.

"It was a promise. Promises have to be kept," she wails.

I reach toward her as far as I can.

CHAPTER THREE

Nine days, one hour until the deadline.

Then I hit the floor. I've tumbled out of bed and knocked my chin on the nightstand. I sit up with a start and rub it. I blink and look around. Early morning paints our room with soft dapples of sunshine. My hand twitches. I locate a pencil that rolled under my bed and shake off the dust motes clinging to it.

The pencil connects with paper, and the girl from my dream materializes in my sketchbook. I try hard to capture the effect of the wind in her hair and the desperation on her face. My hand moves rapidly over the paper, as if an unknown force controls it.

Sweat beads at my temples, flattening the tiny hairs against my skull. I suck my lip under my front teeth, and when I stop drawing I touch my finger to my bottom lip and bring it back stained with a drop of blood. I smear crimson across the bottom of the drawing. More DNA, just like the hair I let loose for the birds.

I stare at the drawing long and hard. Something is missing, but as much as I wrack my brain, I'm at a loss. A door to a dark room in the back of my mind that was opened a crack slams shut. Something is not right.

The coat calls to me like a mournful moan as I get ready for school, but I ignore its pull and reluctantly leave it hidden beside my bed.

When Patty and I approach Brandonville Middle School, we see groups of kids huddled around the front steps, hurtling jeers like sharp pebbles down the street. A seriously nerdy newsboy cap sails above the crowd, only to be caught and sent flying in another direction.

The hat soars through the air again. Taj. He runs back and forth, desperately trying to retrieve his hat. Every so often, one of the kids will let him get close enough to let his fingertips graze the brim, before sending it just out of his reach again. A look of desperation clouds his eyes. Without thinking, I start toward him.

"Stop." Patty yanks me back.

My heart drums and my hands shake. "I know him, Patty. From preschool. We should do something."

She glances over at the scene, then straight ahead, as if she didn't notice. "Like what? You want them to turn on us?"

I stop, planting my feet. "It just doesn't seem right to ignore—"

"The world's not perfect, Maggie. Preschool was a long time ago." She tugs on my arm, pulling me off-balance. "Let's use the gym entrance."

I stumble after her, turning back to glance at Taj. I've seen the look in his eyes in someone else's eyes before. As I turn away from him and follow Patty around the corner, my heart is heavy.

The first two school periods crawl by. There is no way I can concentrate. My stomach rolls in queasy waves when I think of how I hurried away from Taj when he was in trouble. But I have to remember what is important. Finishing my painting.

I can't stop thinking about the tweed coat and my dream; my bones seem to actually ache for the coat. Third period I have art class, my school sanctuary, a place where I can let go of numbers, dates, spelling, and anything else bothering me, and relax in a zone of creativity. The turpentine-laced air soothes my senses. I've always been at my happiest when surrounded by the scent of paint and the dust of charcoal.

Ms. Cherry, my art teacher, finishes setting up a still life composed of silver bottles and a bunch of pale-blue hydrangeas, when a dark-haired boy knocks on the door frame and hands Ms. Cherry a pink slip of paper. Taj.

My heart skips.

His too-short khaki pants bunch at his ribs where they are cinched by a woven belt. Hung on his thin frame is a pinstriped black vest with a silver pocket watch chain hooked on a button. The chain loops down to disappear into his left pocket. Under the vest he wears a white dress shirt, its sleeves pushed up with black elastic bands. Around his neck dangles a pair of leather-and-brass goggles.

His legs and nutty brown arms are thin and gangly, almost spider-like. His face is long and mournful, like a Modigliani portrait. But his eyes—dark, large, and soft like a puppy dog's—warm me inside. Topping his head is the dirt-smudged newsboy cap. His style is a far cry from the jeans and hoodies most boys at our school wear.

When he sees me his face breaks into a smile.

My table partner, Kathy Lundy, nudges me with her elbow and whispers in my ear, "Oh my God, follow fashion much?" She nudges me again. "Look at him smile. Somebody thinks he has a chance with you." She giggles so hard she has to stuff her hand in her mouth to stop the noise.

I scrunch up my nose. "Him? Are you crazy?" I feel bad about my words, but they fall out of my mouth before I can stop them.

"I know, right?" She flashes me a kissy face, which ends up making her look like a nauseated goldfish.

I roll my eyes, then sink into my seat and wish myself invisible.

"Class, let's welcome Taj Mabibbi to our circle," Ms. Cherry says.

Bored mumbles of "Hi, Taj," echo around the room, along with unkind whispers that fill quiet corners.

"You know what this means," Ms. Cherry says enthusiastically, her pink-frosted lips forming a wide grin.

Everyone moans, which makes Ms. Cherry smile more. She has a crazy obsession with astrology, and since we sit in pairs at our tables, she insists that our partners be the best astrological matches to maintain calm and harmony in her classroom.

"Taj, may I ask your birth date?" Ms. Cherry tosses back her unnaturally black, stick-straight hair and pulls out her big book of charts.

Taj looks around, unsure. "I'll be fourteen on June fifth."

"Hmmm, Gemini," she murmurs as she consults her lists. "Yes, we need to make a slight adjustment." She taps the paper with her long, aubergine-lacquered fingernail. "Kathy, my little Pisces, why don't you swim on over and sit with my dear Taurus, Michael. And Michael, don't give her any bull." Ms. Cherry slaps her leg and laughs. The entire class moans again.

She slides her finger down the class roster. "And Taj, please take a place next to my lovely Aquarius, Maggie. Maggie, can you raise your hand so he knows who you are?"

He strides toward me before I even respond. Everyone turns and stares. At that moment, I wish I could disappear into the tile floor. Kathy winks at me and moves to her new seat. I make a sad face, wave goodbye to my former neighbor, and slump down into my chair. Taj takes his seat next to me. "Just like old times, Maggie."

My head still down, I smile. I catch a whiff of cinnamon, and then notice the package of Red Hots sticking out of his back pocket. He sees me looking at his butt and grins. Really? Oh, no. The warmth creeps up my neck.

By the end of the day I've drawn dozens of sketches of the tweed coat, but they all look forced, boring. Still my hand won't quit. I pull my backpack out of my locker. Someone taps me on my shoulder and I jump, dropping my heavy pack smack dab in the center of my big toe. It immediately throbs.

"Miss McConnell, you're still planning on entering the Peabody Summer Arts Academy Competition, correct?" Ms. Cherry adjusts the silver silken scarf that holds back her black hair. "Have you started anything?"

"Well, I was going to do a portrait of my cat."

"Pedestrian, you can do better." She huffs. "I realize your moon sign is at a low but it should be rising soon. I just know you're going to make me proud."

"I'm working on it, Ms. Cherry." My face gets hot and I can't look her in the eye. All I've produced so far is total crap.

"Looking forward to seeing something magnificent. Remember, make sure you get it to me by next Wednesday morning, ten sharp. I'm driving the entries from our county up to the judging committee myself. The director is a Leo. Very compatible with me." She winks, then pats me on the shoulder and continues down the hall.

Wednesday. Less than nine days.

The coat. I spent all night trying to paint that thing, and it turned out to be an utter mess. I'm spending too much of my precious time thinking about it, but I can't help it. It's like a mosquito bite I can't stop scratching.

Even though it pains me, I realize the coat is holding me back. I need to focus. I can dump it in the trash after I go home, but every cell in my body shouts *no* at the thought. Perhaps I'll pack it away and store it in the basement.

Brisk air ruffles my hair as I bike the three blocks to Silver Lake Home for Seniors for my three-hour-long volunteer shift. The Victorian mansion rises into view like a grand old lady. Painted three shades of pink, she stands out like a frosted cake between the small brick ranch houses crowding her sides.

I prepare to lock my bike to the front step's railing, but then I stop. Going inside will mean losing time I can spend on my contest entry. I decide to call and say I'm sick. But before I can turn and speed away, the double front door groans on its hinges and opens. Immediately I'm enveloped by the lily-of-the-valley-scented perfume of eighty-five-year-old Miss Berk. She waves me in.

Snagged. I snap my lock closed and follow her inside.

Miss Berk's snowy white hair is carefully twisted into a neat bun that rests on the top of her head like a crescent roll. I'm not surprised to see her; she always waits for me at the front door on the days I volunteer. It's one of the few things she remembers these days.

I first noticed Miss Berk's mental decline after I rescued Seurat from under the home's porch. Miss Berk and I were sitting in white wicker chairs trying to think of a good name for the abandoned kitty. When I scratched the cat's speckled head, his markings reminded me of the hundreds of tiny dots used in pointillism.

I asked Miss Berk if she thought Seurat was a good name and she turned to me, questions in her eyes. That was the first time I saw the faraway expression that she now wore so often on her face. For the rest of the afternoon she was convinced I was her childhood friend, Freyda.

"Freyda, I thought you'd never get here." Miss Berk closes her gnarled hands around mine. Yep, she's out of it today. Great. It's going to be a long afternoon.

"It's me. Maggie," I say, giving her hand a gentle squeeze. I should just play along as her friend from the past, but for some reason I want to bring her back. Keep her with me.

She smiles, and a distant look clouds her dove-gray eyes. "I thought we might be able to get some knitting done today. I know how much you love to knit."

I pull my arms out of my navy peacoat and hang it up in the hall closet. "Afraid I don't know how to knit, Miss Berk." Before shutting the closet door, I stuff my hat in my coat pocket. "But I'd love to do some sketching or maybe watercolor painting with you." I push up my sleeves, ready to work. Maybe I'll find inspiration here the way Degas found inspiration in ballet studios.

A tall mirror stands at the end of the hall. I catch a glimpse of my reflection and my body fills with ice. My image is changing. My face thins out, the skin draws taut over my skull. My cheeks hollow and my eyes sink deep into their sockets. Knobby elbows protrude from skeletal arms. I try to hide their ghastly appearance by pulling down my sweater sleeves.

My heart races, and the hair on the back of my neck bristles. Dad was reduced to this state before he died. Nothing but skin and bones.

Horrible thoughts invade my mind. Is this how it started for Aunt Bridget? Will my world break into tiny pieces the way hers did? A shiver starts in my toes and ladders up to my shoulders. My birthmark itches again. I paw at it like a flea-ridden cat.

A hand on my shoulder makes me jump.

"Hey, Maggie, what's new? Besides a Greek letter, of course." The girl pushes back her hair, her honey-blonde bob catching the light. "Sorry, lame one, but I thought I'd at least get a little snort or even a tiny chuckle out of you. You're always so serious." She gives me an exaggerated frown.

I rub my eyes, and when I look again the scary image in the mirror is gone. A shudder shakes my body. I squint at the mirror one last time. "Uh, hi, Suzi. Didn't see you." Suzi Valentine is the director's granddaughter. She's a senior in the high school the next town over. Sometimes she comes to help out in the office.

"Oh come on, how could you miss me?" She slides her hands over her curvy hips. "I know. I know. You'd call me Rubenesque."

"I—"

Miss Berk steps in front of Suzi and taps her foot. "Oh, Freyda, you were always the most clever knitter. Come into the parlor. I have my knitting bag all prepared."

Behind Miss Berk's back, Suzi twirls her finger next to her head. "Come into the parlor, said the spider to the fly," she whispers. "I don't know how you do it, girl." She winks, "Catch ya later," and hurries off to the office.

"Sure," I say, still a little shaky. "See ya." What the heck just happened? Maybe the school nurse can give me an eye exam.

"Come on, then." Miss Berk hooks my arm in hers and leads me into the parlor. "You'll catch your death of cold if you stay much longer in this drafty old foyer."

With one last backward glance at the mirror, I let her lead me away.

"Sit down, Freyda." Miss Berk nods toward the couch.

No use trying to convince Miss Berk of my true identity tonight; she's firmly stuck in another time.

Mrs. Valentine, the home's director, crosses the hall carrying a big cardboard box. With her round, cherub-like cheeks and cupid-bow mouth, she certainly lives up to her name. Mrs. Valentine sets the box down in the doorway and nods toward it. "Suzi's been helping me do a bit of early spring cleaning. You know I can never say no when the residents want to use my attic for storage, but now it's starting to look like a hoarder's lair. Afraid it's a fire hazard." She eyes Miss Berk's knitting bag. "Poor dears can never seem to part with anything."

I know how they feel.

"Looks like you're getting right to work."

I nod and give her the thumbs-up sign.

"Your envelope with a little something in it is on the desk, dear."

"Thanks, Mrs. V."

Miss Berk taps my shoulder. "Freyda, I remember how much you love the color blue."

I actually do like blue, but so do a lot of people. *And, my name is Maggie*, I want to shout.

"I have some lovely blue chenille yarn in my bag." Miss Berk digs through her rose-covered carpetbag. It reminds me of the kind of bag Mary Poppins carried. I wouldn't be surprised if Miss Berk withdrew a big, black umbrella, but all she pulls out is yarn.

Miss Berk hands me a pair of long needles and a soft, round ball of yarn, then pulls a skein of yarn and needles out of the bag for herself.

I hold the needles awkwardly in my hands and shrug. "I'm sorry, but I really don't know how to knit. Are you sure you wouldn't rather paint?"

Miss Berk lets out a barking laugh like I told her a good joke. "Of course you do. Cast on. Like this." She loops and twists the yarn onto one of the needles, her old fingers surprisingly nimble. I follow her example.

Soon I catch the rhythm and am able to keep pace with Miss Berk. My fingers seem to have a mind of their own—like they actually *have* done this before. It's kind of odd how well I can knit.

As our needles softly click, my mind keeps drifting, skipping like a pebble over a pond. Miss Berk's childhood stories. My painting. The tweed coat. The contest. Dad. Aunt Bridget.

"Are you not feeling well, dear?" Miss Berk asks, her hands still.

"Sorry, I've got a lot on my mind today." I didn't notice my foot twitching until she spoke.

"Such as?" She tilts her head like a bird, watching and waiting for my answer.

"Well, I'm entering an art contest to get a scholarship to go to this really awesome art school in Princeton this summer."

She pats my leg. "You should have no problem, you're a wonderful artist, dear."

"But I haven't finished anything to submit yet and it's due in less than nine days." I sound like a big whining baby but I can't stop. "And, there's another thing. I bought a coat the other day at the thrift shop. A tweed coat with a black fur color. I thought it might be an inspiration, but—"

Miss Berk's knitting falls to the floor and she grips the edge of the sofa. "What exactly does this . . . this tweed coat look like?"

I bend to pick up her needles and smack my head on the edge of the coffee table. "Oww." I rub my forehead. "It's gray tweed with a mink fur collar. Inside is a tag with the letter P on it."

"Paris. The coat was probably manufactured in Paris," Miss Berk says softly. She sometimes seems so sharp. Her eyes are clear. She's back.

"Hmmm. Never thought the tag might say the name of the place it was made. It makes sense, though." I'll Google Parisian manufacturers when I get home.

"Don't you remember when our fathers went together to Paris on business and brought back all of those wonderful gifts for us, Freyda?"

She has slipped away from me again. Bye, bye Maggie, and hello, Freyda.

"And don't worry about the deadline, Freyda. You never missed a deadline. It was always me that missed them, remember?"

The grandfather clock in the hall gongs six times. I lay my knitting on the table and stand to go. Miss Berk catches me by the arm, her bird-like fingers strong as steel talons. "Please wear the coat next time you visit, Freyda. I want to see it."

"But it's distracting me from the painting. I think it best if I get rid of—"

"You must never get rid of it. I don't understand how you could even consider doing that. It was a gift. Promise me you'll keep it."

"I don't—"

"Promise me." Miss Berk has a wild look in her eyes.

"Okay, okay. I promise." A voice deep inside the recesses of my mind repeats the word "promise" over and over.

A shiver ripples through me.

CHAPTER FOUR

Eight days, thirteen-and-a-half hours until the deadline.

At home Mom hunches over the kitchen table with bills spread out in front. Dad's wedding ring hangs from a chain around her neck, still sparkling the way stars do eons after they are extinguished. Even though it makes me sad to see Dad's ring hanging from a chain, I feel comforted that Mom is not ready to forget him, either.

With red, puffy eyes she looks up at me, her gaze slightly unfocused. "Your plate's in the microwave, Maggie." She stuffs a check into an envelope. "Make sure you turn off the bathroom light when you go t'bed. Electricity's not free, y'know." She frowns and purses her lips as she writes another check.

I hang my peacoat and wool hat on the hook by the back door. Reaching into my back pocket I take the twenty Mrs. Valentine gave me and place it on the table. "Here, Mom."

"Oh, darlin' you don't need to."

"I want to."

Mom's frown softens. "Thank you, darlin'."

After scarfing down my dinner like a starved dog, I escape to my room, pull out the tweed coat, and slide my arms inside. The satin lining tickles my bare skin and the fur brushes softly against my neck.

The coat's scent wafts around me—cedar with hints of sugary vanilla and roses. I've never been much of a perfume girl—that is Patty's thing—but now I wish I could bottle this scent and dab it behind my earlobes every morning.

I walk to the mirror hanging on our closet door, the Silver Lake mirror incident still fresh in my mind. Everything looks normal. Slowly, I button the velvet buttons and smooth down the black fur collar. I stand back and observe my reflection.

The hem of the tweed coat grazes my kneecaps and the sleeves fall past my wrists to the edge of my knuckles. Patty was right. It *does* look like an old lady's coat. I was hoping it might look okay and I could actually wear it outside the house. Maybe it looks better from a different angle. I turn sideways and stare. Nope. Frump-city.

Something flickers behind me.

Lights dance in the mirror.

But when I spin around, nothing is there. *Probably the headlights of a passing car.* I turn back to the mirror and see it again. Eight sparkling glimmers of light all in a row. The yellow lights flicker like eight candles burning behind me. A fog settles over my body. I try to see through its filmy cloak but my vision fails. *I should know those lights. I should know what they mean.*

Goosebumps pop up on my arms and the tiny hairs on my neck stand up. A shiver shakes my shoulders and the birthmark under my collarbone itches like mad. Music drifts into the room. And laughter. Soft laughter intermingles with excited conversation.

I twist around, hoping to catch something in the act. But nothing is there. When I turn back to the mirror, the lights are gone and the room is silent again.

I creep over to the window, pull back the curtain, and peer out. Nobody wielding flashlights. No alien ships hovering over the front lawn. No gangs of people walking home laughing and talking. Nothing.

Just my imagination? Or?

I glance one more time in the mirror. Still nothing.

I need to stay away from mirrors.

Maybe I really do need an eye exam.

I drop onto my bed. Patty probably has the television on downstairs, and my tired eyes must be playing tricks on me. I wish I could rest, but there is no rest for those wanting to win an art scholarship. I have to finish my painting. But first I need to do a little research.

I do a quick computer search for Parisian manufacturers, and come up empty. Since Paris is one of the fashion capitals of the world, the list of Parisian designers is super-long. And really, I'm not even sure what I'm looking for. Parisian coats with magical qualities able to hypnotize the world's most uninspired artist?

With my hands tucked in the coat's pockets, I slip into Dad's studio and stare at the painting I worked so hard on yesterday. I hope it might look better to me tonight. It doesn't.

I flip through the pages in my sketchbook for ideas, and Dad's memorial card slips out. He smiles up at me from the small photograph and my stomach tightens.

"Dad," I croak out. I miss him so much. If he were here, he'd be able to tell me exactly what to do to win this contest. I can't figure out anything without him.

I place the card between the pages of my book again and return to my room, hiding the coat, then sliding my sketchbook under my mattress just as Patty joins me.

She studies me, her face turns sideways. "You okay, *chica?*"

"I don't know," I answer. I don't want to talk about Dad with Patty. It hurts too much. Plus, she'll just lecture me about moving on. I can't understand how she can forget him so easily. Instead I say, "I'm worried I'll never get my painting done for the art scholarship."

She lets out her breath. "Don't sweat it. You'll probably work like crazy the night before it's due, but you'll get it done. You always do. Plus, I'm sure Ms. Cherry has other work you've painted in class that you could enter, right?"

"Probably." But none of them are scholarship caliber. I pull my blanket up to my chin. They are pretty, as in a painting that matches a room color or picks up the designs in a sofa. Not the type of painting people ponder over, trying to guess the story it holds within its brushstrokes.

Patty clicks off her bedside lamp and plunges us into darkness.

"Love you much, Patty," I say.

"Love you more, Mags," she answers.

We've been saying good night to each other like this since we were little girls. I guess some habits just stick. It's a familiar routine that keeps you grounded when everything else falls apart around you.

When I hear Patty snoring, I pull my sketchbook out from under my mattress. Seated on the edge of my bed, I sneak out Dad's memorial card again and hold the small piece of stiff paper under a patch of silver moonlight. I can almost hear him talking to me, "No worries, darlin'. 'Twill all work out in the end."

I lean closer to the square of light, and my sketchbook slips from my lap. It hits the floor and lays open to the page where I sketched the portrait of the girl wearing the tweed coat in my dream. She looks so sad. Just then a gear shifts and something clicks. I know what to paint!

When I open my eyes, early morning sunlight softens the edges of everything around me like watercolors blending from one color to the next. Easels blur against the walls behind them—

Easels?

I look around and see turpentine cans, paint tubes, brushes. I am in Dad's studio wrapped in the tweed coat, curled on the floor next to my easel and clutching a wet paintbrush.

I sit up, blinking to focus my sleep-filled eyes, my bones stiff from spending the night on the hard floor. Seurat paces back and forth, his crooked tail twitching like a metronome. Outside, clangs and clunks announce the garbage men emptying trashcans.

I turn toward my easel and let out a gasp.

Big brown eyes stare back at me from my canvas. The coat girl.

My horrible attempt at painting the coat was scrubbed away with a turpentine-soaked rag that's draped over the edge of the easel, and a sepia sketch of the coat girl is in its place. She wears the tweed coat, and although the portrait is only from the shoulders up and unfinished, I can see the tip of something on her left lapel. A patch?

My hands tremble. I stick them under my armpits to still them. Did I paint her? But I have no memory of it. Am I truly going nuts? Will I wake up minus one ear, Van Gogh-style, tomorrow?

On shaky legs, I grab my sketchbook and the coat, and then firmly shut the studio door, tiptoeing back to my room.

Footsteps sound in the hall. I shove my sketchbook under my mattress and stow the coat under the covers. Patty strides in, bathrobe belt tied around her waist and a wet towel flung over her shoulder. She runs grape-scented styling gel through her hair with her fingers while humming a song. "So what have you been up to?"

"What do you mean?" I snap. Did she see me last night in my zombie state? Did she tell Mom?

"Chill, Mags. You've been awfully tense lately. You were up and out of bed before me today. You never wake up earlier than me."

My shoulders relax. Good, she didn't see anything. "Oh, um, I was getting some work done on my painting before school."

Patty pulls her shiny hair into a high ponytail. "Oh, okay, Georgia McKeeffe."

"O'Keeffe," I murmur.

"Whatever." She clips a crystal-encrusted barrette into her hair.

After we dress, she raises our bedroom shade all the way up to the top, letting in the morning light. Dust sparkle-dances in the sunshine.

I want to tell her about my dream and my painting, but the words stick in my throat. I can't push them out no matter how hard I try. They are trapped.

After she leaves the room, I pull back the blanket and stare at the innocent-looking tweed coat at the foot of my bed. All this weirdness originated with its purchase. I remember all the stories Dad told me of haunted rooms, haunted paintings, and haunted statues in Ireland. We'd whisper when we talked of such things, because Mom forbade it. But it always fascinated me.

I hop on our boxy, old computer that Mom trash-picked from one of the offices she cleans at night, and type in "ghosts." As I scan the Wikipedia entry, one line stands out. "Ghosts are generally described as solitary essences that haunt particular locations, people, or objects."

Ghosts can haunt objects. It is true. My gaze flicks toward the coat.

27

My left eye twitches. I push the coat down in the space between the wall and my bed and cover it with my blanket. My eyes can't seem to leave the lump it makes.

The air in my bedroom grows thick, my breath quickens, my heart pounds. I grab my backpack, throw on a sweatshirt, and dash out the door.

At school, rushing to Ms. Cherry's art class, I slide into my seat just as the second bell trills. That's when I notice the still-life display in the center of the room: tall black boots.

A tingle starts under my left collarbone, then spreads, pinging from my birthmark to my eyeballs and blurring my vision. My ears fill with the crunch of boots marching. *Clump, che-clump, clump, che-clump.* An acrid, sickening, hard-boiled egg smell fills my nose.

"Wow, just like old times," Taj says as he settles into his seat. "The dynamic art duo together again."

As I gulp back the Pop-Tart I grabbed for breakfast, I feel a light tap on my arm. "You don't look well. Are you okay?" Under the brim of a brown derby, Taj stares at me; his eyebrows are pinched, and concern darkens his eyes. "Sorry for the cliché, but you look like you've seen a ghost."

I suck in my breath, struggling to maintain my composure. I avert my gaze from the boots. "Ghost?"

I shake my head to clear it. The memory of the coat girl's face surfaces, and again I remember Dad's ghost stories. Banshees, pookhas . . . But they were just silly stories, weren't they?

"Do you believe in ghosts, Taj?" My voice trembles. I drop my gaze and stare down at the desk.

"Absolutely." Taj's charcoal stick scratches across a large piece of newsprint. "The way I see it, all life forms are composed of energy, right?"

I raise my head and nod, relieved that he doesn't think my question totally wacky.

He continues, "Well, you can't dispose of energy; you can just displace it. It has to go somewhere after we die."

Sounds reasonable. Not crazy at all. And if what he says is true, can I find Dad's energy?

Taj's pocket watch tick-tick-ticks. Looking into his eyes now, I notice they are golden brown, like the color of the sweet sun tea Mom makes in the summer. My heart flutters, catching me by surprise. Is it possible the ice that froze my heart three years ago is beginning to thaw? But that ice keeps me locked and safe, frozen with Dad. If that ice melts, does that mean Dad's memory will slip away, too?

I survey the room. My old seatmate, Kathy, and her new seat partner, Michael, have their heads together, furtively glancing at me and whispering. I glare at them.

Ms. Cherry taps me on the shoulder with her bony finger, and I jump. She arches one of her black, painted-on eyebrows. "Pour yourself into your work, my Aquarius the water bearer." She picks up a long, skinny charcoal stick and hands it to me. "It's time to get serious. Contest deadline is looming, my dear."

My mouth twitches, but I can't smile. Ms. Cherry's finger has left a dusty mark on my shoulder, and while brushing it off, I catch sight of the boots. A wave of nausea rises again and I turn away. I decide to draw the light fixture instead. With hesitant, choppy lines, I outline my drawing.

"Did you ever hear the theory that, um, energy can go into an object and make it, um, haunted?" I whisper to Taj.

Ms. Cherry clears her throat. "I may have to check my star charts for you two," she says with a wink. Across the room, Kathy giggles. I furrow my brow and smudge back one of my lines.

"Can we talk more about this later?" I stare at my paper. "I mean, if you have time, not that I want to take up all your time or anything."

He turns his charcoal stick on its side and shades a portion of his drawing. "Lunch period?"

"Okay," I say, my nerves twisting. Patty won't like him joining our lunch table.

I go back to my hideous drawing, which ends up looking more like the ashes of a stamped-out fire than a light fixture. My stomach is tighter than an overstretched canvas.

CHAPTER FIVE
Seven days, twenty hours until the deadline.

Lunch. My stomach flips. Taj will be here any minute. If only he would take off the hat and some of his odd accessories, maybe the girls would think he's okay. But I have a feeling Taj cares very little what others think of him. How else can he wear these crazy outfits? It won't bother me to sit with Taj; I know the girls at our table just tolerate me because I'm Patty's sister, but Patty will be furious.

He said he believes all life forms are composed of energy. Will he sense the frantic pulse of my energy? Can I keep its electric thrumming down to static level until the girls finish eating and go to the bathroom to reapply their makeup?

I hurry to our table and duck down.

From behind a pillar, I see Taj enter the cafeteria and scan the room, then take a seat by himself on the other side. I'm safe for the moment, but I really do want to talk to him.

Sugar Reed, the queen bee at our table, eyes my tray. "You want to split the brownie?" she asks. "I'll give you the apple my mom packed."

"You can have it." I toss her the brownie. She'll make me give it to her anyway. Plus, my stomach is still not quite right.

"Thanks." She takes a huge bite, and a flurry of crumbs sprinkle the front of her pale-blue sweater like ashes falling across a clear blue sky.

Ashes. Smoke stacks. The thought makes me shudder.

She sees me staring at her.

"What? Nothing wrong with dessert first," she says with a frown.

I squirt ketchup on my cheeseburger. Across the room I catch Taj looking at me; I tense up and squeeze a little too hard. The tiny packet explodes out the side and splatters the table, Jackson Pollack style. Sugar gives me the evil eye, then inspects her sweater for ketchup stains.

I wipe the table with a napkin, then try to force down my cheeseburger. Between bites, I steal glances of Taj.

Patty's elbow knocks me in the ribs.

"Who do you keep looking at?"

"Huh?" Am I that obvious? "That boy over there. The one with the hat. He's the guy I went to preschool with." I nod in Taj's direction. "I feel bad for him. He must be lonely."

"The new guy?" She glances his way. "Look at him."

"What's up with the hats?" Sugar asks. "I mean, someone new to our school should try to blend in and not deliberately wear weird stuff to make himself stick out."

Everyone at our table looks over and nods in agreement.

Patty shifts back to me. "Concentrate on Ethan Wilson." She motions toward the other side of the cafeteria, where two boys cute enough to be in a boy band munch on burgers and fries.

Ethan and Aiden Wilson started attending our school earlier this year. They are brothers, less than a year apart and in the same grade, just like Patty and me. The day Patty set eyes on them, she decided they would be perfect boyfriend material for us.

I sneak another look at Taj. He's reading *The War of the Worlds* by H. G. Wells as he spoons lime Jell-O out of a cup. As if he can sense me looking, he lifts his head and waves me over. I lower my eyes and concentrate on folding my straw wrapper back and forth into a tiny accordion.

Patty tugs on my sleeve and whispers, "He's waving at you now. Just ignore him." Her pretty forehead crinkles.

I glance at Taj in his white tailored dress shirt with thin green stripes, and his purple-and-green paisley vest. He's watching me from under the brown derby; it sits cockeyed on his head, its odd leather band covered with tiny brass gears. A monocle hangs around his neck. "He's my desk partner in art class. We were talking and . . ." My voice wavers. I clear my throat and speak with more confidence. "He's not so bad."

"You can't take in every stray you meet, Maggie. People aren't cats."

She frowns back at him, and then her eyes bore into mine. As soon as Sugar gets up to grab a straw for her juice, Patty says, "Stay clear of him, Mags. You hang with him and before you know it, people will think you're weird, too. It sucks, but that's how it works around here." She nibbles on her tuna salad sandwich, and then turns to me again when Sugar returns. So everyone can hear, she says, "By the way, Sugar told me that she heard from Mary Feltman that Aiden Wilson might like me."

She blasts a movie star smile my way, perfect except for the chunk of celery sticking between her teeth.

"You got something right here—" I motion to my mouth.

She ducks, covering her teeth and scrubbing the bit of celery away.

"Is it gone?"

I nod.

"Anyway, once I start going out with Aiden, I'll hook you up with his younger brother, Ethan. We can double-date at the Spring Fling!"

"OMG, you two with the Wilson boys would be so cute," Sugar squeals.

The Spring Fling is the biggest dance of the year. Patty has been planning for this event since September, but I dread it as much as she hates hanging out with me at art gallery exhibits.

Patty is as smooth with boys as the manicured tips of her fingers, but I chew my nails down to the quick. I say the chances of me being asked to the dance—even with Patty's help—are zero to nil, anyway.

I steal a few more peeks at Taj when Patty isn't looking. Butterflies do a crazy flutter dance inside my stomach.

Okay, weird coat-buying compulsion, spooky dream, unconscious nocturnal painting, and now I'm crushing on this odd boy.

He catches me looking at him and smiles. My cheeks, I know, are turning the color of Patty's strawberry yogurt. I hang my head so my hair shields my face and busy myself gathering the trash on my tray. When I look back, he's gone.

I got through today's lunch, but what about tomorrow? Will I invite Taj over to our table? Will I leave my sister and the others and join Taj? I wonder if he is on Facebook. I wonder if he'll accept my friendship.

I sneak away to wander around the cafeteria's courtyard, kicking through dried leaves, searching for the bright greens and purples of crocuses pushing up through the cold ground. Returning, the way bulbs do every spring. If only Dad could return like those dependable blooms. Sitting on a cold concrete bench, I stare at the gray sky. Then I jump. I didn't hear Taj until he sat down next to me.

"Sorry," he says. "Thought you might like some company now." He flashes me a lopsided grin as he shrugs his shoulders.

I rake my hair back. "I was thinking and I didn't hear . . . I mean, I didn't see . . . well. Sorry about lunch. I—"

"No, problem." Then he looks straight into my eyes, which turns my spine to jelly. "But next time, I'm coming over to your table."

I laugh a little too fast and a little too loud, while also noticing how blindingly white his teeth are.

"Don't worry. I know I'm an acquired taste."

"It's not that, it's just Patty is trying to fix me up with this boy and—"

"Lucky guy." He slides a pencil behind his ear.

"Lucky guy" meaning Taj likes me? Or "lucky guy" as a sarcastic way of saying I am a jerk? Given my behavior, the second answer is more likely.

"This is an excellent thinking spot. What were you thinking about, if you don't mind me asking?" He tips back his hat.

The answer of death seems too morbid. "Not much. Just looking to see if any crocuses are blooming yet."

He shifts slightly on the bench. "Ah, spring bulbs. Not one of my favorite topics."

"Why? Are you more of a winter person?"

"No." He stares at the ground for a moment. "Well, it's a situation that started when we moved and I entered my new elementary school. As you can tell, I don't always have the easiest time fitting in. But things weren't so bad." He stops talking and stares at the ground again.

"So what do flower bulbs have to do with school?"

He turns and looks at me. I can see the gray clouds reflecting in his eyes.

"My father is a mortician, and my mom's occupation is making my life hell." He laughs stiffly.

My stomach clenches when he says mortician, but I try to ignore it.

"Maybe I'm being harsh. Anyway, at Easter time, people bring potted flowers to set at the gravesites. The groundskeepers leave them there until they die."

"Yeah, I know all about that." My mother brings my father yellow daffodils every year. Yellow was his favorite color.

He stops and looks at me questioningly, then continues. "Well, when the flowers die, the groundskeepers toss them into the rubbish."

"They do? That seems like such a waste. Why not plant them?"

He laughs again, this time more easily. "My mother would like you. That's exactly what she thought. Every year she rescued them, wrapped them in newspaper, and planted them in our garden the following year."

"Your garden must have been beautiful in the springtime."

"It was. A cacophony of color. But she was running out of room to plant things. Then she heard about the PTA's school beautification project."

"So she donated them."

"Exactly. And everybody loved it until one of the moms found out where the bulbs had come from and what my dad did for a living. Well, word went around the school."

"And what happened?"

He clears his throat. "The flowers bloomed, and some of them, especially the hyacinths and narcissus, were particularly fragrant. Some clever kid deemed them the smell of death, and by virtue of association I was given the same label. When I walked by, they'd say something like, 'Do you smell that? Death just walked by.' Or they'd hold their noses when they were around me. I've got a thicker skin now, but it really bothered me as a little kid."

"That's awful. People can be so cruel." And then I remember myself at lunch. I should apologize.

"Some, but not all. I try to associate with the kind types." His dimples wink at me.

"Taj, I, I mean . . . " I stutter.

"So tell me about your ghost business. That is what you want to discuss, correct?" he asks.

Just then, the bell rings.

"I gotta hurry. My next class is on the other side of the building. Where's your next class?" I ask, my face volcanic.

"That would be study hall, library, B wing," he reads off his schedule.

"That's where I'm going, too. You can walk with me if you want. I mean you don't have to but—"

"Sure, lead the way."

I struggle for something to say as we walk, but my brain has turned to applesauce.

We hurry to study hall, my head down, hair swinging in front of my eyes. I've never checked out our library's paranormal section, but maybe I'll find a good book on ghostly phenomenon.

As we enter the library, Sugar, resident gossip queen, casts a squinty eye at me. I pretend I don't see her. I'm sure, by the end of the day, Patty will be filled in on every detail of my arrival to the library accompanied by the odd, new boy.

I duck behind a bookshelf and sit at the last table in the back of the room. He parks himself next to me.

I want to talk to him, but the librarian, Mrs. Finch, watches us, her finger itching to cover her pursed lips. "Can't talk here," I whisper.

"Shush," she says, right on cue.

The computer's list of library books in the paranormal section contains all fiction. No serious books. The same PTA parents who think reading Harry Potter will lead to a generation of witches and devil worshippers must have banned the supernatural from our library.

I return to the table empty-handed.

Taj pushes his brown derby farther back on his head and passes me a note.

Sorry to unload my past problems on you. So, tell me about this haunting of yours.

I look around the room. I don't know if it is just me, but it seems like every person in the room has stopped what they were doing and all eyes are trained on us. Patty's warning of me being considered "weird" by association rings in my ears as images of daffodils and tulips crowd my brain.

"Oh, the ghost stuff?" I squeak out. "I can't believe you fell for that. I was just messing with you. You didn't think I was serious, did you?" I edge away from him and fake a little cough. "Might not want to sit too close to me. Think I'm coming down with something."

"SSHHHHHssh," the librarian reprimands me again.

Self-conscious, I pull out a notebook and start doodling, losing myself in my drawing. Before long my squiggles and dashed lines begin to resemble the tweed coat. This coat seems to be wheedling itself into every fiber of my being.

"Hey, your artistic skills have dramatically improved since pre-school. You should submit something to the Peabody Summer Arts Academy Competition."

I look up; the librarian is in the hall talking to a group of students. "How do you know about Peabody?" I ask, staring, mesmerized by the swirling purples and greens in his paisley vest.

"I'm working on a sculpture to enter."

I stifle a giggle and whisper, "So you've graduated from finger paints to sculpture, impressive."

"Very funny." He draws a silly face on my paper.

I raise my gaze to his. He may attend Peabody with me if I get in? A tiny thrill zips through me. "I've been trying to work on a painting to enter for weeks."

"Excellent." His dimples deepen. "Total serendipity."

"What?"

"Serendipity. Our meeting again. A fortunate discovery made by accident."

My face's furnace rises to its highest setting. I lower my eyes and pretend to be engrossed in my work. We have so much in common, Taj and I. More than any of my so-called lunch table friends. He may be the perfect person to share my ghost mystery with.

"Taj, I need to talk to someone about some weird stuff—"

I am about to confide in him when I catch sight of the school custodian, Mr. McHale, climbing a ladder, spare light bulbs in hand. A barbed wire tattoo encircles his bicep. A fence. My God, *not the barbed wire fence! High-pitched wails rip through the room, screaming, moaning.*

A loud roar drones in my ears. My vision narrows toward a pin of light. The musty smell of old carpeting fills my nostrils.

The last thing I feel is my head hitting the floor.

CHAPTER SIX

Seven days, eighteen hours until the deadline.

I pass out in the library and am taken to the school nurse. She feeds me crackers and orange juice and rants about crash diets and girls' unhealthy obsessions with being super-skinny. Okay, maybe I'm not eating much of my lunch, but I try to reassure her that I'm not barfing in the lavatory or counting calories. Even so, she makes sure I get the complete nutrition lecture before she lets me go back to class.

I open my locker, and a note written on a green piece of construction paper flutters out. I quickly pick it up and read:

Would like to talk to you more about your ghost. Meet me at Evergreen Cemetery after school. I think it would be quite an appropriate place to talk about matters of the supernatural.

~ Taj

My stomach dips. I desperately want to know more about this ghost business, but the last time I was in a cemetery, my world had just fallen apart. I'm not sure I can handle it, but I have to know. I already plan on stopping by the thrift shop after school to see if they can tell me who donated the coat. Then I'll hurry to the cemetery.

Brass bells jingle when I pull open the door and step inside. At the register, the gum-smacking cashier slides her eyes over me, then goes back to reading her dog-eared paperback.

I watch her eyeballs move back and forth as she reads her novel. When she gets to the end of the chapter, she sticks a ripped piece of cash register tape in the spot, looks up, and scowls. "Yeah?"

"Hi. I bought a coat here a few days ago and I was wondering if you could tell me who donated it." I twist my fingers as I talk. She never even blinks.

"No idea. You can ask Mrs. Biggs if you want," she says, monotone.

"Great," I answer with fake enthusiasm in an effort to win her over.

She opens her book and bends her head, dismissing me.

I look around. I don't see anyone. "Um, do you know where she is? Mrs. Biggs, I mean?"

She groans, not looking up she says, "In her office."

I smile. "Um, could you please tell me where it is?"

She places her finger in her book and glares at me. "Through the double doors in the back and up the steps."

"Thanks!" I call, hurrying in the direction of the doors.

"But you can't go up there," she yells.

I stop, mid-stride.

"Employees only. You'll have to wait until she comes down." She snickers.

I browse in the aisle closest to the doors leading to the office, glancing back at the cashier every so often, but she keeps her eye on me. *Go back to your stupid book,* I shout in my head as I pretend to shop. I don't have time to wait. If I don't go to the cemetery soon, Taj may think I bailed on him again and leave. For once I wish I had the cell phone. But I don't have Taj's number anyway.

The bells clink on the front door.

Someone's shoes shuffle toward me. The person mutters. I smell talcum powder and wintergreen. I turn, slowly. A yellow-toothed smile greets me.

It is the old lady I swiped the tweed coat from.

I rush farther down the aisle.

She keeps coming. Shuffle, scuffle. Mutter, mumble.

A dead end. I face the wall.

I keep my back to her. The shuffling footsteps get closer.

There is a tap on my shoulder. My heartbeat picks up its pace.

A rack of dresses stands between me and freedom. I shoulder through them, and wire hangers clatter to the floor in my wake. Just need to get through these double doors. One . . . two . . . three. I bolt forward and pound up the steps toward Mrs. Biggs' office.

I push up my sleeves. Long pink welts crisscross my arm from the wire hangers I dodged through. I rub my fingers over them. At least they didn't break the skin.

I stop at the door, smelling vinegar. It brings me back to Easter time at our house when I was younger. I envision Dad carefully pouring white vinegar into a row of six teacups, and then dropping a fizzing PAAS tablet into them. Patty and I each had a half a dozen hard-boiled eggs to decorate. She would drop her eggs into the cups of dye, taking all the space. I grabbed crayons and drew intricate patterns on all my eggs before dipping them in a variety of colors to create a tie-dye effect. Dad turned and examined every inch of my crazy creations, complimenting me on my creativity. Patty's eggs sat drying in her carton, saturated with color, untouched. Did he make too much of a fuss over mine? Is that why—

"Can I help you?" Mrs. Biggs is eating a salad out of a plastic container while reading *People* magazine. She shoves a plastic fork full of lettuce in her mouth.

"Hi. I was in a few days ago. Bought a coat. I'm trying to find who owned it before me."

"I see." She taps the fork on her front teeth. "Well, most people leave their donations by the back door. Unless there's a name inside the coat, it'll be close to impossible."

My feet stay planted. I can't leave.

She pushes away her salad. "What's wrong, honey? Go on, tell me about the coat. Maybe I saw who left it."

"Well, it's tweed. Has a black fur collar, um, kinda old looking—" This is a waste of time. I should leave. She'll never remember.

"Tweed with a fur color? Swing coat style? Yes, I do remember it. Poor woman had a truckload of donations. Cleaned out her attic." She puts her finger on her chin. "Let's see. A sweet woman. Bright-pink lipstick. Young girl with her, I believe. Afraid I didn't catch her name, but I know she was local." She tears a piece of paper from a notebook on her desk. "Leave me your name and number. She said she'd be back. If I see her again I'll give you a ring."

I scribble down my information. "Thanks."

"Can I ask why you're so interested?"

"Just curious," I blurt out as I back away. I don't think telling her the coat is possibly haunted will play very well. "Thanks for your help." I run down the steps and out the back door.

It isn't a home run, but it's not a total miss either.

Now I need to hurry home and get the coat.

Then off to the cemetery.

CHAPTER SEVEN

Seven days, sixteen hours until the deadline.

I plan to grab the coat and scram. Patty has a Student Council meeting after school, but they don't usually last long, so I have to be quick if I want to avoid an interrogation.

Opening the squeaky back door as quietly as I can, I scan the room. Kitchen is empty. I tiptoe through the deserted living room, climb the stairs, and slip into our bedroom. I gather the coat in my arms and hug it like a long-lost friend, taking a big, relaxing whiff. Then I carefully fold it, place it in a plastic bag, and nearly knock Patty over as I fly down the stairs.

"Whoa, what the heck—" Patty yells.

I keep going, not stopping to talk. No time for questions. I hop on my bike and race to the cemetery, peddling like a mad woman.

Sweaty and out of breath, I drop my bike at the iron-gated entrance and unhook the bag from my handlebars. The afternoon sun dips behind a cloud, and winged angels, crosses, and rows upon rows of tooth-like gravestones cast long shadows on the barren ground. The trees in the distance are black claws slashing the sky. The wind picks up my hair and flings it in front of my eyes. I gather it back behind my shoulders. The sky darkens; the air hangs heavy with the sweet smell of wet earth. Storm is coming.

My mind's color wheel turns as I translate the landscape before me on canvas. I would paint this scene in black-and-white with spare brushstrokes, like a Japanese ink drawing. Maybe I'd use some purple in the deep shadows. I can just about picture it in my head when my internal color-mixing monologue is interrupted by a loud *caw*.

I jump and spin around.

A crow eyes me from his vantage point on top of the black iron fence. He clutches some sort of bug in one of his razor sharp claws. *Prometheus Bound*, comes to mind. I saw the painting last summer at the Philadelphia Museum of Art and was both repelled and fascinated by the depiction of an eagle ripping out the liver of poor, chained-up Prometheus.

"Hiya, Maggie," Taj says, and tips his hat.

I jump again. The crow squawks and flies off, dropping its prize.

Taj picks up the bug, examines it, and says, "Amazing. Rhinoceros beetle." He holds it out so I can see.

I bend closer. The walnut-size beetle's horn appears dagger-like. "Interesting. My dad and I . . . I mean, I collect stuff like that to draw."

He holds the dead beetle out. "Want it?"

"That's okay." What kind of weird girl will he think I am if I accept the bug? What kind of weird boy gives a girl a dead bug in the first place—even if I do think it is kind of cool-looking. Although, his definition of weird will probably be drastically different than the normal population's definition.

He pops it into the pocket of his long, black duster. The wind gusts, and he tugs his brown derby down more firmly. "Would you like to sit? I know a perfect place."

I wipe my sweaty palms on my jeans and follow Taj. The plastic bag on my arm containing the tweed coat swings like a pendulum as we trail along a twisted path through the cemetery. I can't help thinking of all the bodies resting just beneath our shoes in the cold ground. Mothers, fathers . . .

Fathers who are missed. Fathers who are needed by their daughters.

My eyes tear up and I think I may lose it, so I desperately try to think of something else. I look up at the sky. Colors. What colors would I mix? Base of white, dab of cerulean, pinch of dioxazine purple . . .

Finally, Taj points out a creamy white marble bench under a huge sycamore tree, whose thick limbs reach like graceful arms across a fenced-off fresh gravesite. I turn away from the upturned dirt.

The skin under my left collarbone stings as if an army of red ants is having a picnic. This darn birthmark is really bothering me lately and I should probably see a dermatologist, but I don't want to add to Mom's pile of bills. I try to ignore it.

"Have a seat." Taj gestures to the worn marble bench.

I perch on the edge and feel a chill through my jeans. "So, remember when we were talking about your ghost theories?"

He nods, and his dark hair shines blue in a shaft of light breaking through the clouds.

I pull out the tweed coat. "This is it. My haunted object."

He is quiet as he examines it.

I pick up a curled brown leaf and tear off little sections until it is all stem and veins, then toss it to the ground as I wait for Taj to speak.

This is nutty, and now my story will start to verge on crazy-town. "There's something about the coat," I say, hesitantly, "I can't explain it, but it calms me—kind of like when I was a little kid and carried around my baby blanket. Just the smell of that tattered thing made me forget all my problems."

"A security blanket."

"Right. But there's more." I brief him on the girl in my crazy dream, the painting, and the strange reaction I had to the boots in art class today. "I think the girl in my dreams once owned the coat and is trying to send me a message."

Taj tips his derby back on his head, the brass gears glittering in the waning light. "A classic case of a haunting, in my opinion."

My shoulders drop with relief. "That's what I think, too."

Taj's eyes blaze bright. "I can't resist a good mystery. In fact it's my favorite genre to read, after horror and science fiction." He hands back the coat. "So we have on our hands a bonafide preternatural coat?"

"Preternatural?"

"Sorry, been reading too many Dean Koontz novels. Preternatural is one of his favorite words." He flashes me a bright smile. "It means supernatural or haunted."

I nod, petting the coat's fur collar, sparks of longing springing from my fingers. "Coat looks pretty normal, right?" I run my hands through my hair. "My sister Patty would think I'm crazy. In fact, lately I've been leaning toward that possibility, too."

"Then your sister Patty would be wrong." Taj's eyes search mine. I notice tiny flecks of gold glittering in the dark pools of brown. One day I want to paint his portrait.

"Do you think we can figure out what this girl wants to tell me?"

He pats my arm. "Indubitably."

Pings of happiness shoot up and down my body; the spot where he touched me tingles.

"Actually, I was thinking that perhaps we should have a séance and try to contact the coat's ghost." He pulls a book out of his army-green messenger bag and taps the cover, which reads *Adventures in the Paranormal.* "The book gives instructions."

A séance. The word sends my mind into a spin. After Dad died I was so desperate to talk to him. The last week of Dad's life I sat by his side night and day, wiping his brow when fever burned him from the inside out. I held his hand and talked to him softly when invisible demons taunted him, reminding him of everything he'd never accomplish.

I was determined he would not die alone. I would not allow it. But I was only a ten-year-old girl, too young to keep such a big promise. I didn't get much sleep that week and longed to curl up for a few minutes on my soft mattress with my squishy pillow. Finally I caved, telling myself I'd take a short nap while Dad was resting comfortably. I woke to Mom's sobs and my heart froze. Alone, he had slipped away from this world.

Desperate to apologize for leaving him and hoping to be able to say goodbye, I bought a Ouija board and planned on holding a séance to try to communicate with him. To tell him I was sorry. Mom found out and flipped. I'd never seen her so angry. When Taj said the word séance, I saw my mom making the sign of the cross and heard her voice ringing in my ear, "Jesus, Mary, and Joseph! I will not have you bringin' the devil into my house, Margaret May McConnell." She took my board out to the yard, dumped it in a metal trashcan, and burned it. As the flames licked the side of the can, my hopes of ever contacting Dad again floated away like ashes on the wind.

What was I doing here? For all I knew, Taj's family was a bunch of devil worshippers looking for a new recruit.

Above me the sycamore's long limbs look sinister, ready to grab me and stuff me in a grave. Its pale bark peels in long strips; I imagine decaying flesh. My heart races. I can't catch my breath. My birthmark goes from an annoying itch to a fiery burn.

A crow lands on top of the tombstone in front of me and caws, its screech loud and accusing. Its beady golden eyes stare at me threateningly. Edvard Munch's painting *The Scream*, shrieks in my head; its swirling blacks and oranges tighten around my throat.

"No, Taj. I can't do a séance with you," I choke out. "I gotta go." I throw the coat over my shoulder and take off running.

I stumble over the winding path, not knowing if I'm going in the right direction. Lightning cracks in the distance, thunder rumbles, and then the sky opens. Raindrops pelt the ground and mud spatters the hem of my jeans. I tuck the tweed coat into the plastic bag and wrap it tight, holding it to my chest, slipping on the now-muddy path and catching myself from falling by grabbing hold of headstones. My heart pounds; names on the headstones crowd my vision. All these people. Gone.

The path ends. A fog rolls in and veils the landscape in a velvet white mist. I can't locate the cemetery gate. Behind me something shuffles in the brush. I turn, and stare into two glowing eyes.

"No!" I tear across the grave-studded field. Marble angels reach out, trying to catch me in their cold grasp. Lightning cracks again and I see the dog's body silhouetted by the light. It blocks the cemetery gate. Thunder rattles the ground.

I turn and run, my arms still wrapped around the bag holding the coat. A depression in the earth makes me lose my footing and I fall flat on my face. I try to scramble to my feet when pain rips through my leg and pins me to the ground. Teeth. They pull at my flesh, tear at me . . .

"Maggie!" Taj shouts.

I turn my face upward. Cold needles of rain sting my cheeks. Taj stands over me with his hand extended. By his side sits a golden retriever; its tail swooshes back and forth. "Let me help you."

I swat at his hand. "Get it away from me!" I yell. "It's biting me."

"What's biting you, Maggie? I don't see—"

"Get it away!"

Taj looks left and right. "You mean Trixie? Are you scared of her? She's really friendly."

"Noooo, get it away!"

"It's okay, calm down." He points. "Home, Trixie."

The wet dog bounds across the field and disappears. Taj bends down and holds out his hand again. "Let me help you."

I ignore it, spring to my feet, and dash out the gate, not looking back. His "sorry" catches in the howling wind.

Not stopping to grab my bike, I run; my wet hair whips my face and my feet slap through puddles. Head down, I jog in the street, keeping to the middle of the road to avoid the torrents of water gushing out of clotted gutters.

The squeal of tires causes me to look up. Lights blind me. They've caught us. The involuntary thought triggers panic. I scan the area, looking for a place to hide.

"Maggie!"

I turn back in the direction of the lights. Headlights. A car pulls up beside me. "Maggie, get in."

"Suzi?" Suzi sits behind the wheel of her grandmother's big white Cadillac. "I'm all muddy," I yell. The wind almost steals my words.

"Leather seats. Mud wipes off. In."

With shaking fingers I open the door and slide in.

"Jesus, Maggie. You scared the crap out of me. I almost hit you."

"Sorry," I mumble and my breathing slows. It's only Suzi from Silver Lake, I keep telling myself. My heart continues to rattle my ribcage.

Suzi punches the gas, and I slam back in my seat. "Whoops." She looks over at me, then turns up the car's heater. The hot air warms my icy skin. "So what brings you out on this lovely night?"

Another crack of lightning splinters the sky. Thoughts of séances, devils, and vicious dogs whirl through my mind.

When I don't answer, she says, "Gram's getting a new car and giving this old girl to me. Couldn't resist a short drive to test the brakes on this boat. Didn't know it would be a life-or-death test. Where were you coming from?"

"Had to meet someone."

Suzi chuckles. "Say no more. He had to be pretty darn cute for you to come out on such a crappy night." She slides her eyes over me. "What were you doing, mud wrestling? Looks like you forgot your bikini."

"I fell in the cemetery."

"Oh." She pauses. "Oh, wow. Sorry. How are you? Things getting better?"

Trapped in this two-ton hunk of steel and leather, I am not ready to discuss Dad, especially with Suzi, a girl I only see occasionally. My feelings about Dad are mine and mine alone. I can't share them. Putting them out there will somehow dilute them. "That's my house. The yellow one on the left." I unhook my seatbelt, preparing for a quick getaway.

"Listen, don't worry about it. I know we aren't close, but if you ever want to talk . . ."

She stops and I jump out of the car.

"You need anything, call me. Suzi's Service available 'round the clock."

I nod and jog to our back door.

Still in one piece, my pain safe within me.

For now.

CHAPTER EIGHT

Seven days, fourteen hours until the deadline.

Patty lounges at the kitchen table reading *Seventeen* magazine and twirling pink bubblegum around her finger. She glances up at me and the magazine slips from her hand. "Hey, Mags. What the heck were you up to?"

I look down at my mud-encrusted clothes. "Got splashed by a car."

"What a jerk." She picks up the magazine again and turns a page. "So, what was up earlier? You almost knocked me down the steps." She blows a big bubble and pops it with her little finger.

"Sorry. Had to get a book back to the library before it closed. Otherwise it would have been overdue and I'd get a huge fine." Wow, that lie fell out of my mouth way too easily. Luckily, Patty has no idea the library doesn't close until eight o'clock.

She glances up again. "What are you doing with that ugly coat?"

The sleeve of the tweed coat hangs out of the bag. "My art project," I mumble as I hurry upstairs.

I strip off my wet, muddy clothes and pull on a pair of sweats. Before dressing, I examine every inch of my leg. Not a single tooth mark.

Seurat follows me to the laundry room in the basement. I drop the bag with the coat on the floor and transfer the clothes from the washer to the dryer. The wet clothes chill me as I set the dryer to tumble. I dump my muddy clothes in the washer with a cupful of soap.

I scan the boxes packed away in a corner. Dad's books. I pull off the lid of the one tucked in the back. These are the books Mom wanted Dad to get rid of. She feels they are an insult to the Catholic Church. But instead he hid them between the furnace and the sump pump. I pull out the books and read the titles until I find the one I am searching for, *Ghosts and the Paranormal*. I swipe the dust from its spine. Maybe I'll find some answers here.

The air in the room grows cold, freezing my lungs with each inhalation. Lightheaded, I head back to the laundry area with the book and sink to my knees next to the coat bag. Leaning my head against the wall, I scratch the birthmark under my collarbone and watch the drum spin. The red, blue, and green colors drain away, twirling faster and faster until I am left with only shades of gray.

The grainy, gray world I see before me is like an old-fashioned black-and-white movie. I spy the dark-eyed girl hanging sheets in a dreary yard. Long lines of white sheets billow in the wind like swaying ghosts. There isn't a patch of grass in sight. I move closer and watch.

White air curls from her chapped lips. She clips the last pin to the sheet and sticks her hands in her mouth. When she pulls them out, the blistered surfaces glow red.

"The painting is going well?" she asks, grabbing the corner of another sheet and bringing it up to the clothesline.

Turning to me, her eyes wide, she says, "Remember. Promises should never be broken." She crosses her hands and places them over her heart. "Remember Gittel."

The landscape swirls again in the dryer window. "Wait, who's Gittel?" I shout, but her image fades and the shades of gray brighten to swishes of color.

With Seurat sleeping next to me on the basement floor, I stare at the clothes going 'round and 'round in the dryer. The tweed coat is draped over my shoulders, the plastic bag is discarded by my side, and the book is by my feet. Thing is, I don't remember taking the coat out of the bag. Two words keep repeating in my mind: "painting" and "Gittel."

Upstairs, I hide the book under a painting cloth, drop to the studio floor, and fold my legs underneath me. Shivers prickle my insides like cactus needles, and I wrap my arms around myself.

From the painted canvas on my easel, the coat girl's big brown eyes plead for help.

"Are you real? How do you know about the painting?" My voice trembles. "I want to help you, but I don't know what you want me to do."

Down the hall, my sister sings. Her voice lifts and falls smoothly; melodies come easily to her. Guiltily, I realize I haven't talked to my sister about what is happening to me. She is my best friend. Yet, I hide my sketchbook and don't share my dream or the other odd things that are going on. I wonder if Aunt Bridget ever talked to Mom about her demons. If she had, could Mom have helped? I shouldn't be confiding in someone I barely know, like Taj. I should tell my sister. I glance back at the painting, retrieve Dad's book on the paranormal, and leave the studio.

Dad's book contains some interesting stories. Dogs barking crazily at something no one can see. Sheets pulled off beds. Appliances that turn on in the middle of the night. Green orbs darting throughout a house. Weird noises and soft whispers heard through baby monitors. The people recounting their stories seem pretty normal: postmen, nurses, mechanics. The more I read, the more convinced I am that the coat may actually be haunted. The book even details how to hold a séance. Maybe I should have stuck it out. Wonder if Taj will give it another go, or has he already written me off?

Later that night I lie under the covers, rehearsing what I'll say to Patty. She's pinning up a picture of her latest movie star infatuation—some blond guy with eyes an unnatural shade of cobalt blue. Satisfied that her hottie is positioned just right, she pulls the big cardboard box where she keeps all her mementos—photos, report cards, love letters—out from under her bed, slides it into the middle of the floor, and tips the lid off.

She kisses the photo of the guy who was demoted from her wall, "Sorry, baby, I'll never forget you," and places it in the box. Shuffling through the papers, she oohs and ahhs over her past loves, then pulls out a piece of pink construction paper. "Remember this?" She holds the paper up so I can see. A kid's drawing of a little girl. "Remember when you wanted Mom to change my name?"

"I did? Did I draw that?"

"Yep. Wanted to call me Rebecca." She points to the bottom of the page. "See, you even wrote it on here."

I don't remember the drawing.

"Thank God, Mom didn't listen. Can you imagine? People would have probably called me Becky." She scrunches up her nose. "So not me."

"Or Becca?"

"Huh? Yeah, I guess, maybe Becca. Now, I might have gone for Sonia, or Tatiana. Cool names."

I like the sound of Becca. It reminds me of someone nice.

Patty places the lid back on the box and shoves it under her bed, then hops up and slides under her covers.

The tweed coat is wedged between my bed and the wall. I grab hold of its sleeve to give myself strength. "Can we talk?"

Her bedsprings creak as she rolls over on her side to face me. "What's up?"

I clear my throat and croak out, "It's the tweed coat."

"You still trying to paint that ugly thing? Why don't you paint a pretty vase of flowers? Lots of people would like that." She leans up on her elbow.

"Maybe." I stare at the ceiling, watching the dancing shadows cast by the trees outside our window. I try to formulate the words I practiced in my head. "Here's the thing. Remember when I came home with the coat and you teased me about the fur?

I thought it was weird, too, but I just *had* to buy it. And, since then, strange things have been happening to me."

"Strange, how?"

"I've been having really crazy reactions to normal things."

"That's common. It's called stress." She checks her pink fingernails for chips. "Omigod. Mags, are you stressed about the Spring Fling? I told you I'm working on the Wilson boys. Have faith in your sister. We'll snag them."

The Wilson boys are the farthest thing from my mind. "And, I had a dream about the girl who owned the coat before me." For some reason I leave out the part about the clothes dryer. "She wants my help." I pet the fur on the collar. "I think the coat is haunted."

Patty flips her white sheet over her head, then back down. "Boooooo!" She shakes with laughter. "Haunted? Come on, seriously?" She clicks off the light. "You okay in the dark or do you want me to leave the light on?" She giggles.

"Taj thinks so, too," I say quietly.

Patty stops laughing; the moonlight streaming in the window makes her eyes flash green.

"You mean that weird boy you knew when you were, like, three or four? You told *that* guy all this stuff?"

"He believes me."

"That's because he's crazy. Now go to sleep." With her face to the wall she adds, "Better stay away from him. People might get the wrong idea."

"But he's an okay guy, Patty."

"He's no Wilson brother."

"But—"

"Drop it, Mags."

I don't know what else to say. It's useless to argue with her. But I know one thing, she can't tell me who I can be friends with. Hopefully Taj still wants to be my friend after the way I treated him and his dog earlier.

Patty waits in the prickly silence for me to say good night. "Love you much, Patty," I say, my voice flat.

"Love you *more*, Mags," she answers, firmly.

I turn and face the wall. If I told Dad my story, he wouldn't have laughed. He'd have wanted to help me. Tears escape the corners of my eyes and drip down into my mouth, filling it with salt.

Before long, soft snores come from Patty's side of the room. I can barely take a deep breath. Maybe she *is* right. It might be stress.

But I don't think so.

I can feel it in my bones.

Something is going to happen.

Chapter Nine

Seven days, nine hours until the deadline.

I try to sleep, but the coat whispers to me again, "Paint, Maggie. Paint." Helpless to resist the urge, I pull out the tweed coat and sneak into Dad's studio. I grab an old towel and stuff it under the door so the light won't be seen in the hall. "We don't want any interruptions," a voice in my head warns.

I look at the tweed coat draped over a chair. Why did I bring you? I know I'm not going to attempt painting the coat again. But, perhaps . . . slowly, I push my arms through the sleeves and pick up a paintbrush. A soothing heat ripples through my body, filling me with warm confidence. The tight cord wrapped around my chest loosens.

Mixing burnt sienna, cadmium red, and titanium white, I work in the colors on the coat girl's face with sure brushstrokes.

"Tell me who you are. I'll try to find you." I stare into the painted eyes as I work. "Everything will be all right. I'll help you."

I continue to paint, whispering words of encouragement and comfort.

Referring to the sketch by my side, I shade her cheeks full and rosy. Her eyes, raw umber and a hint of burnt sienna, are dark and big. I take extra care with the brown curls that fly about her face like a smoky halo. Using a touch of titanium white tinged with ultramarine blue, I highlight the strands so they jump off of the canvas.

One last stroke of my brush, and I'm finished for the night. I step back from the easel and think about Dad. I know I have something. I'm not sure what, but I know it is special, and Dad would have agreed. Less than eight days left. I'll have to paint quickly, but it isn't impossible.

After cleaning my brushes, I pull the coat off and hold it close. The soft fur collar tickles my cheek as I breathe in its comforting scent of vanilla and roses. I sneak back to my room and stash it beside my mattress.

The sky has turned from midnight blue to violet. I close my eyes and yawn, suddenly exhausted. Maybe I can get a few hours of sleep before school. I roll toward the wall. Like a magnet, the coat seems to draw me near. I am finding it harder to leave it during the day.

The next morning, I wake up to the weather reporter announcing a wind chill temperature in the teens—unusual for March. Snow flurries are even predicted. I drag myself out of bed to peer outside. That's when I see it. A pair of handprints silhouetted against the spider web of frost on the window. I creep closer to get a better look. Tiny rivulets of moisture fall like tears from the prints' outline.

"Watcha lookin' at?" Patty grabs her silver makeup bag, ready to head to the bathroom.

"Did you do this?" I point to the prints.

Patty squints. "Oh come on, you can do better than that. I still don't believe in ghosts, Mags."

"But I didn't do it," I snap.

"Put your hands on it, then."

Slowly I place my hands on the window; the prints fit like a pair of gloves.

"Really? How dumb do you think I am?" Patty turns and leaves.

"But—" The bathroom door clicks shut.

Was it me? But I just woke up.

With my hands pressed against the glass I gaze at the street below and shiver.

What is happening to me? Is this how it started for Aunt Bridget? I wish I could talk to Mom about her.

I dress, my heart thundering, my mind whirling, I have to get a grip.

Then I remember last night's wonderful painting session. The coat! No one can blame me for wanting to wear a fur-collared coat today.

I slide my arms into the sleeves. Like little fires, my worries are snuffed out as calm envelopes me.

Finally able to take a deep breath, I snuggle into the tweed coat. My artistic inspiration—and something much more. I hurry downstairs.

"Maggie May, what is that old thing you have on?" Mom asks. "You and Patty look so cute in your matching navy peacoats."

I brush the soft, black fur against my chin. "Got it at the thrift shop. Vintage chic. Thought I'd try something different."

Mom runs her fingers over the fur collar. "It'll be warm for sure, but it looks like an old woman's coat, Maggie. I really think you should put on your other one."

I stuff my hands deep into the pockets. "I think it looks kind of cool. I'll ask Patty what she thinks."

Mom continues to stare at me like I have two heads. I reach up and touch my skull; the way things are going lately, I can't be too sure.

"Are you losing weight, love?" Her eyebrows draw together and a look of concern shadows her face.

"New diet," I say. Why did I just lie? I never lie to Mom. I can't tell her I've barely been eating. I sure don't need her and the school nurse on my case. Nor can I tell her I've been compelled to stay up all night painting.

"Diet? You have a lovely figure, darlin'." Mom tsks her tongue and grabs her quilted parka. "You are okay, dear, right?"

"I'm fine, Mom."

Loaded buckets in hand, she heads toward the door. "Okay. Well, I've got the car warmin' up. Gotta go. See you at dinner, fashion plate. Try not t' starve yourself. Love you."

"Me, too. Bye, Mom."

The door closes.

Starve? A hot poker stabs me under my collarbone. The room spins. My knees go weak as I grab the wooden banister. A metallic garbage taste fills my mouth and I gag.

By the time Patty pounds down the steps, I regain my balance. She stops on the landing and lets out an ungodly shriek. For a moment I think she stepped on Seurat's tail.

"You are not going to wear *that* to school," Patty screeches, pointing her finger at me.

"It's cold today . . . the fur."

"Seriously?" She cocks her head and pushes past me. "Maggie, it's weird-looking. Our friends will talk."

"Get real, Patty. They're your friends. You go to the mall with them. You sleep over at their houses. You go to all their parties. And I don't care if they talk about me."

"Oh, come on. You're always invited, but you always say no. It's not my fault. Anyway, we are all friends, and I do care what people say about you. What if Ethan sees you in it? What will he think?"

I brush my chin across the fur. "I don't really care what he thinks." As soon as the words leave my mouth, I regret them. Patty only wants to help me, to share the things that come so easily to her. "Sorry," I mumble.

She glowers at me, then stomps out the door, leaving me with a chill even in the fur-collared coat.

There is no way she can understand my feelings for the coat, and how grateful

I am that it is leading my art in a new direction. But Patty is right about the fashion part—that is her area of expertise.

Taking two steps at a time, I run upstairs to the bathroom and grab the tube of calamine lotion from the medicine cabinet to swipe over my itchy birthmark. Although, the annoying itch seems to have calmed on its own.

I brush my fingers over the stubbly tweed, thinking about the way Miss Berk reacted to my telling her about the coat. She wants to see it and I want to know what else she'll say about it. I reach for my peacoat hanging on a hook by the back door. I pull one arm out of the tweed coat, but then stop. I can't.

I have to wear it.

CHAPTER TEN

Seven days, thirty minutes until the deadline.

I don't think I'll be able to function at school until I see Miss Berk again, so I take the long route past Silver Lake on the way.

On the front porch of the nursing home, Miss Berk rocks in a wicker rocker. She is all bundled up in a crocheted afghan. I approach and her face crinkles into a big smile.

"I didn't expect you this morning." She shakes her head and furrows her brow. "Have they told you not to come to class anymore? I heard that was happening."

"What?"

"There are rumors flying about." She flings her hands around. "It's not safe. But let's not speak of it. What shall we do today?" Miss Berk's eyes hold the misty look of the past. "Your coat looks very snazzy. Do you like mine?" She holds out her arms and the afghan slips down past her shoulders. She's isn't wearing a coat. "Papa says the green compliments my eyes."

I don't know what to do, so I play along. "It's very pretty."

"Come closer." She sniffs the air. "Mmmm. Chanel Number Five. Oy, the boys will be flocking around you today." She giggles, then stops and holds up her index finger. "But remember, Samuel is my beau." She sighs. "He's such a dreamboat." Miss Berk claps her hands. "I cut out the dress pattern you lent me. I can't wait to start sewing, although my stitches will never be as straight and even as yours."

Her blanket flaps in the cold breeze. I bundle her back up as best I can. "You should get inside. It's kind of cold."

"Yes." Miss Berk glances down the street. "Papa said we should stay indoors." She rises, hunched. "But not for too long. You know how much I love to run in the fields. I can't wait until summer. We'll have a grand time again."

She grabs hold of my arm and I lead her inside. "Yes, we always have fun, Miss Berk." I give her hand a squeeze. It must be so hard to grow old and confused. But perhaps going back in time is like a vacation for her. An escape from her frail body.

"So, who do you have your eye on this week, Freyda?" She giggles. "You are so lucky, all the boys are gaga over you."

I can't help but laugh. As if. But I continue to play along. "There is one boy I kind of like."

Miss Berk motions for me to sit with her on the sofa. "Is it Benjamin, the butcher's son? He is quite handsome."

I flop down next to her. "No, he's a new boy at school. But I think I may have messed things up with him. I don't think he could ever like me."

"Nonsense. You are a catch, and if he doesn't realize it, then he's not good enough for you." She pats my hand. "Let him get to know you. He can't help falling for you."

"You think?" It almost feels as if I am having a heart-to-heart with a real girlfriend.

"I know," Miss Berk says with a firm nod.

I glance at my watch. Oops, three minutes before first bell. "Okay, well, gotta run to school. I'll see you later."

I hoped Miss Berk would have been more with it and been able to tell me something about the tweed coat. At least my visit may have given me one more clue. Chanel Number Five. I don't know much about perfumes, but I know someone who does. If she is still talking to me after this morning.

I shuffle down the hall wearing the tweed coat. As Patty predicted, the coat doesn't go over well. People turn and give me strange looks, but I don't care.

I hate to take the coat off and stuff it in the cramped metal prison of my locker, but what am I going to do, carry it around all day? That will totally steam my already-angry sister. I give the coat a pat, then shut my locker door, rattling the metal to be sure the lock is secure before hurrying to my first class.

Just knowing the coat is nearby relaxes me, and I spend the morning doodling possible backgrounds for the coat girl's portrait. The doodles would look so much better if I was drawing them while wearing the tweed coat, I think.

I stride down the hall to art class, no longer frantic about letting Ms. Cherry down. Taj heads my way. I want to apologize for freaking out on him yesterday. I don't know what got into me. I mean, I love animals, dogs included.

I also can't wait to tell him I've rediscovered my painting mojo. All because of the tweed coat.

Taj's eyes light up when he sees me, and he tips the black bowler on his head in my direction. He hurries his pace, not seeing the foot jutting out from behind a door ready to trip him. Before I can warn him, he goes flying.

Pencils, papers, books—all airborne. Taj lay in a heap on the floor. The laughter around him starts as a light patter and then turns into a full-fledged downpour. Not everyone laughs, but when I catch their eyes, they hurry away. I push through the crowd, picking up his things as I go. When I reach him, I offer my hand.

I recognize the boy who tripped him. Mike Davis, the chief of police's son. He was the same boy who shot paper straw wrappers at me during my lunch period last year. I always pretended I didn't notice. I was afraid if he knew it bothered me, things would have just gotten worse.

Mike steps between us. "What are you doing?" The big oaf tries to block me with his beefy hands.

"I'm helping him up." I move around the jerk.

Mike lets his hands drop. "You're one of those ginger sisters, aren't you? Which one are you?"

I'm surprised he even has to ask. I should think it is pretty obvious which one I am, considering I never wear a stitch of makeup and my hair is as dull as dirty pennies, but when I don't answer him, he turns to the kids still watching. "Sorry, did I just trip your *boyfrrriend*," he draws out the word, almost singing it.

Laughter scalds me like hot water. My face burns, but I keep my hand out to Taj, who finally takes it and stands. "Come on," I say, entwining my arm around his. "Let's get to class."

Between classes, I sneak a note into a slat in Taj's locker.
Evergreen after school? Try séance again? Meet at our place.
~ M
I wrote "our place" without thinking. I finally have an "our place" with a boy, and it happens to be a bench between two moss-covered headstones in a dreary cemetery. I open my locker and fall back under the spell of the tweed coat.

Taj waits for me on the marble bench between "Dearly Departed Harrison" and "In Memory of Our Beloved Anne." "Hey, coat looks good. Very Forties retro."

I look down at myself. "You think? Patty hates it."

"Dress for yourself, not others, is my personal mantra." He pops a monocle into his left eye and squints to hold it in place. "As I'm sure you can tell."

I give an unladylike, snorting laugh.

"Listen, Maggie, I want to thank you again for what you did today, but I don't want you getting picked on, too. We can communicate through notes at school, okay?" Taj looks up at me, no sign of the dimples. "I'm used to it."

I don't know what to say. He is giving me an "out," but it is wrong. Dad would have said, "Follow the beat of your heart, not the beat of the drummer." Taj is a nice boy, and I want to be his friend. Maybe even more. But I am realistic. I know he is probably just fascinated by my ghost story, not me. "Thanks, but I'd rather talk in person to my friends."

This time Taj blushes and fiddles with the buttons on his duster. "Thanks. Oh, and hey, don't worry. I made sure Trixie was in her crate before I came over here. If I'd known you were afraid of dogs, I—"

"But I'm not. That's what's so weird. I swear I thought something was attacking me, but when I went home there wasn't a single bite mark on me."

"Perhaps it was a panic attack? My mom sometimes gets them when she works herself up over me not wanting to be a doctor or a lawyer." He shakes his head. "Parents."

"Your mom's not thrilled with your dreams of being an artist? Join the club."

He puts his hand into the deep pocket of his coat. "I made a little something for you. If you don't like it . . . I mean, you won't hurt my feelings if—"

"For me?"

Taj pulls out the rhinoceros beetle he retrieved from the crow the other day. It's been transformed into a thing of beauty. He opened the wings on the back of its carapace and filled it with tiny gears and intricate watch parts. The insect's tail has been replaced with a delicately carved watch stem and crown. It is now a piece of art. I never thought I'd describe something dead as beautiful, but it truly is. "Poor dead beetle," I murmur.

He sets it in my outstretched hand. "The beetle's soul was already gone. I just transformed the shell he left behind."

"It's beautiful."

"It's what I do. My sculpture. My art."

"I never saw anything like this before. All the tiny gears—"

"It's steampunk style. I did a stint of goth but found it too dreary, so I went steampunk last year."

"What is steampunk exactly?"

"The style's kind of rooted in the Victorian era. Like how people of that time would have perceived the future. Very Jules Vern, H. G Wells-ish. You can find the style in literature, art, and clothing—obviously." He waves his hand over himself with a flourish. "I really got into it. Thus, my fashion sense." He chuckles. "Sometimes I feel like I was born in the wrong era. But enough about my clothes; let me show you something else."

He motions me over to a small concrete building behind the sycamore tree. "Welcome to my studio."

"Your studio?"

"Courtesy of the cemetery groundskeeper. I dispose of the dead flowers at the gravesites, which means I collect them for my mother, and help to pull weeds in exchange. Pretty sweet deal."

"Nice, is it far from your house?"

"My dad's the new funeral director at Bradley's Funeral Home across the street. We moved into the apartment on the second floor."

"You live there?" My throat catches. Dad's body is buried in the graveyard behind the Catholic church we go to every Sunday, but his viewing was in that funeral home.

"I know. You'd think I'd be the one haunted by ghosts, but the house is pretty quiet. I haven't detected anything paranormal yet."

I stand frozen, not even inhaling.

"You okay?"

I can't talk about Dad. Not here. Not now. I let out a deep breath. "Sorry. Just worried about the contest, is all."

Taj holds the door open to the small concrete building. Sunlight filters through dusty windows. He flicks on a light and that's when I see it: a behemoth of a sculpture.

At first glance, the sculpture looks like a desert scene. Three elegant camels tread across a glittering desert floor. The camels are constructed with wire, tiny brass gears, and switches similar to what Taj used to transform my beetle. As I examine the sand, I notice the dunes are actually composed of depictions of bodies, stacked one on top of the other. A desert of humanity.

"Genocide in Morocco," Taj says. "That's the name of my sculpture."

"Genocide in Morocco?"

"Don't worry, most people don't know about it. I'm hoping my artwork might open a discussion, or at least make people think." He touches the end of the camel's nose with a slender brown finger. "It's my homeland, after all."

"It's exactly what the judges are looking for," I say as I move closer to examine the complexity of his project. "Something personal. Something that has meaning."

"So many people have died, and it seems like nobody cares," he says, his voice hard.

"Was your family hurt?"

"Not my immediate family, but I believe we are all family. All humans. You know? We should care about everybody, whether it directly affects us or not."

I stare at the sculpture and see the bodies, heaped, gaunt; overwhelming sadness pulses through me. "I should care," I whisper.

Taj pats my shoulder and I wipe my eyes. "Let's start this séance."

Chapter Eleven

Six days, fifteen hours until the deadline.

Taj floats a fuzzy blanket down to the floor and motions for me to sit. I take off the tweed coat and sit cross-legged on the floor; the coat lies neatly across my lap. I smooth the fur on its collar.

As I try to get comfortable on the chilly concrete floor, Taj takes a candle and a pack of matches out of his pocket. He switches on a flashlight and pulls down the thick green shades.

Taj sinks to the floor across from me and strikes a match. "*Voilà!*" The candle lights up, flashing on the sculpture's bronze and silver edges.

I watch the tiny flame's orange light dance in Taj's dark brown eyes. Goose pimples pop up on my arms, and I rub them to get warm. Taj notices. "Allow me, m'lady." He drapes his jacket over my shoulders.

I lay the tweed coat between us on the red blanket. And, although I really do want to hear from the coat girl, I desperately hope Dad will visit, too. "Let's both lay our hands on the coat while we ask our questions," I whisper.

Taj places the tips of his fingers on the tweed fabric. They are only inches from mine. For a moment I forget about everything else but Taj being so close. But only for a moment. Then I remember I am in the middle of a cemetery trying to contact a dead person through a haunted object. A chill runs through me.

"The book," I whisper, "says it's important to concentrate. I'll try to visualize the girl from my dreams." In the candle's flame I concentrate on the coat girl's face. We stay silent. Waiting. Outside a crow caws plaintively. I push my fingers deeper into the fabric.

"Should we ask a question?" Taj asks.

"Good idea." I take a deep breath. "Are you with us, girl who owned this coat?" I ask in my most serious voice, as wax melts and drips down the candle's sides like hot tears.

The candlelight flickers in the dark room, casting weird shadows on the walls.

"Can you give us a sign that you're with us?" Taj ventures.

Silence.

In my clothes dryer vision the coat girl said, "ask Gittel." "Can you tell me more about Gittel?"

My birthmark tingles. I stare at the candle's wavering yellow-and-white flame, concentrating. It jumps and sputters. Then it seems to grow, larger and larger, whiter and brighter. The room turns on its side and spins, round and round, the bronze, browns, and silvers in the sculpture blend in a spiraling rush; reality trickles away like water through my fingers.

I am crouched between two rows of boxwood hedges, body trembling and my mind in a panic.

Next to me, the coat girl shudders in the tweed coat. Beside her, a girl with straight, honey-brown hair shivers. The new girl wears a deep-green wool coat. They pull tightly on a dirty brown quilt and try to keep warm.

The coat girl begins to speak. She doesn't speak English, but I can understand. She nudges the other girl. "Gittel, we'll make a run for it when the sun goes down. We can hide in the caves."

Tears stain Gittel's face. "The ones we played in last summer?"

The coat girl reaches up with her thumb and wipes a tear from the corner of Gittel's eye. "Yes, the passages are confusing, but I know them well. They'll make a very good hiding place. We can drink water from the river. I stuffed some food in my pockets." She shows her the tweed coat's bulging pockets.

"I'm scared." Gittel muffles her sobs with her hands.

The coat girl puts her arm tighter around Gittel and they huddle together. "We must be strong. We can make it. We—"

A gunshot splinters the silence. Men shout.

The coat girl grabs Gittel's hand. "Run, now!" The pair takes off like rabbits, zigzagging across the field and into dense woods. They trip over vines, roots, weaving through thick stands of birch trees. Water trickles over rocks. They slosh through it without slowing. Caves loom before them. "Quick, inside." The coat girl pants. Gittel squeezes through an opening so small I'm amazed she fit.

The coat girl follows her, then ducks out and turns to me, her dark brown eyes glinting like bronze platters. "A promise can't be forgotten. Now, if you want to finish your painting, you must find Gittel." And then she is gone, the gray tweed coat disappearing with her.

"How do I find Gittel?" I shout, but the scene is already wavering in and out like heat over a tar road.

The candle's flame jumps in front of me, red, orange and blue, rising high, then settling back to yellow. My heart beats fast in my chest; my ears strain for the softest noises, waiting for her answer.

"Maggie? Are you okay?" Taj whispers. He pulls up the shades and blows out the candles, then helps me up from the cold floor.

He guides my arms back into the tweed coat. My heart patters against my ribs, as if at any moment it will fly straight up my throat and out my mouth. The walls of the shed seem to close in and I can't catch my breath. The room seems smaller, like a coffin. Like a coffin being lowered into the ground. Like the coffin holding Dad, shutting him away from me forever. I can't breathe, and gasp for air; odd noises come from deep inside my lungs.

Taj grabs my arms. "Let's go outside."

I lean my forehead against the cold marble of a polished headstone and breathe in and out slowly to catch my breath. My hands tremble.

Taj pushes a stray lock of my hair out of my eyes. His touch is so gentle it gives me shivers. "What happened in there? You had a really peculiar look on your face."

The memory is already fleeing. I try to hold it tight before it disappears. "While I watched the candle, I felt myself spinning 'round and 'round. When everything settled I found myself with the coat girl and another girl."

I squeeze my eyes shut and try to remember every detail. "The other girl was named Gittel. They were hiding from bad men who I think wanted to hurt them. They were planning their escape." I turn and look up into Taj's eyes. "They were scared to death." I felt their fear as if it had been my own.

Taj's dark curls shine purple and blue like raven feathers in the fading sunlight. "Incredible. You actually witnessed this vision during the séance?"

I nod and lean into him. His clothing smells of cinnamon and leather. My breathing slows to normal, and my body warms inside the coat. The coat does its sedative magic and my fingers grow steady. I meet his eyes.

"Gittel was the coat girl's friend. They were both running from the same bad guys. But that's all I know. Not really enough to solve anything." I push the heels of my hands into my eye sockets until my vision fills with stars. "She keeps saying 'find Gittel.' How do I find this Gittel? For all I know she's dead, too." Details of the vision disappear like vapor.

A gravestone topped with a bronze cross shines in a patch of sunlight. *Bronze?* "Wait, there's one more thing." I remember the coat girl's piercing brown eyes with flashes of bronze. I step back and pace; dry leaves crunch under my feet. "The coat girl said I had to find Gittel before I could finish my painting."

"She knows about your painting?"

"Yeah, she mentioned it before, when I saw her hanging clothes. Do you think she's watching me?" I look around and shudder. "Like right now?"

"Hard to say. There's a distinct possibility."

I look around again. Dusk shimmers toward twilight, making everything hazy. A shiver rattles my bones. "Who are you, Gittel? And who wanted to hurt you and the coat girl?"

CHAPTER TWELVE

Six days, thirteen hours until the deadline.

No one is home. I take off the tweed coat and sit in the kitchen, silent except for the ticking clock. On the counter, taped to the top of a Vito's Pizza box, is a note.

Maggie,

Working late. Pizza for dinner. Patty studying over at Sugar's house. Lock the doors. Be good.

Mom

My appetite has abandoned me, but I know Mom will be checking to see if I ate, so I take a few bites, then wrap some slices in a napkin, bury it in the trash, and head upstairs.

I run my fingers over the bumps and grooves formed by the dried paint on Dad's last painting, remembering. Then I settle down in front of my painting.

The séance plays over and over in my head. Did I really make contact with a ghost, or is my mind playing tricks on me? If I truly contacted the coat girl's ghost, there is a chance I can contact Dad, too.

I wonder if everyone who dies becomes a ghost, or are ghosts just the souls who didn't get into heaven—or maybe got lost along the way? I don't think Father Flynn at Sacred Heart Church ever discussed that topic during one of his Sunday sermons. I'm sure I'd remember.

I slip the coat on over my sweatshirt. I can't resist diving back into my painting. With all the colors blocked in, I can get to work defining the shadows and adding the tiny details—like the glints of light in the coat girl's eyes and the blue-white highlights of the fur's individual hairs. The deadline is now less than seven days away.

I cup my hands over my mouth to warm them, then open and close them twice. The stiffness leaves my fingers. Warm and relaxed, I use my palette knife to mix titanium white with a touch of cadmium red and burnt umber before picking up a bit of the color with my brush.

I stretch my hand toward the canvas and feel a sharp shock. Zap. Sort of like when you scuff slippered feet on carpet in the winter and then touch metal. I think about the coat girl's words about finding Gittel before I can finish the painting, and then push it from my mind.

A loud creak, followed by scraping noises, makes me jump. The sounds come again, rhythmic in their pattern. It is probably wind blowing the tree limbs against the house. I have to get a grip.

I swing my arms windmill fashion to loosen them. Blood rushes through my limbs. Gripping the paintbrush, I extend my arm again, determined to make contact with the canvas. Inch by inch, closer and closer, my hand trembles more and more. Just as my brush is about to touch the canvas, I shudder so violently that the brush flies from my fingers, hitting the wall and leaving a splat of beige paint.

I spin around, scanning the room for the coat girl's presence. My bare feet smack the hardwood floor as I pace back and forth in the small studio. I remember the morning I discovered the painting. Did the coat girl possess my body during the night to paint the portrait?

Is she in possession of my body right now, making me tremble so hard I can't paint?

The trees groan, scratching the siding.

One more time. Deep breath. I pick up the brush and reload it with paint. Aim for the canvas. I close in and my hand shoots right, streaking cadmium red across all my hours of hard work.

"Nooo," I scream. Dread circles and settles into my chest. My knees weak, I lower myself to the floor and hug my arms around my body. "No, no, no."

She wants something from me, and she isn't going to let me get what *I* want until *she* gets what she wants. I stare into the coat girl's eyes. "What?" I yell. I rip off the coat and throw it against the wall. I pound my fists on the floor.

Snatching up the coat, I slam the studio door and pound down the hallway. She needs the coat to get to me. I wish I never bought it. If I get rid of it, will she go away?

My bare feet drum down the stairs and through the kitchen. I swing open the back door so hard it hits the wall and bounces back. Outside, cold rain stings my face. I stumble down the back cement stairs to the yard, slipping and sliding in the fresh mud. When I reach the trashcan I wrench off the lid and stuff the coat inside, slamming the lid back on. A metal clang echoes in the black night. With my feet digging into the ground and mud squishing up between my toes, I tilt my head upward, letting the rain wash over me. *I am done.*

Back inside, I twist on the tub faucet and scrub; the water turns as dark as burnt umber. Tiny stones stuck in the mud between my toes flow toward the drain, swirling with the dirt and grime. I keep scrubbing long after the water runs clear and my skin has turned pink and raw. This is my body. Nobody else can have it. When the hot water turns cold as melted snow, I finally stop, dry myself, and go to bed.

The next morning, coughing and sputtering, I wake to a mouthful of hair. "Get off, Seurat," I croak, raising my arm to swat him away. But when I reach up, it's not Seurat on top of me. It's black fur. Mink. The coat is draped over me like a shroud. The same tweed coat I threw into the trash last night!

As though it were a snake slithering up my leg, I fling away the coat and bolt out of bed, stumbling away from the thing heaped on the floor. I keep my distance, staring, daring it to move. How? Could Patty have—? No, Patty hates the coat. She would do a happy dance if she knew I threw it away. Mom, maybe?

My feet itch. When I reach down to scratch, I find them thick with dried mud. There are flakes of dirt between my toes. The hem of my nightgown is speckled with soil. I pull back my covers and find dirt smeared on my sheets. I look at the coat and then back at my feet. My God, did I do this?

My heart pounds like hail on a tin roof. There is no getting out of it. I have to uncover the coat girl's story, or . . .

In the shower, rivulets of dirty water swirl down the drain as I scrub my feet clean for the second time since last night. I leave the coat in my room. My eyes keep guard as I wash, squinting to see through the mist building in the bathroom. Is she out there?

Back in my room, the coat is still on the floor where I left it. I poke it with my foot. Nothing. I pick it up, fold it, and lay it on my bed. The coat's scent wafts into the air, relaxing me. It really isn't the coat's fault. It is the girl.

I stride into Dad's studio and stare directly into the coat girl's eyes. "Look, whoever you are, I'm really sorry some bad people were after you, and maybe they hurt you, but that doesn't give you the right to come here and mess with me. You want my help? Well, you better let the coat go back to helping me."

Last night I didn't have a single dream. I slept so soundly—except for the fact that apparently I trudged through the mud in my nightgown and retrieved the tweed coat from the trash. I walk closer to the painting so that the coat girl's nose and my nose are only inches apart. "I'll help you, but you have to let me paint. Understood?" I turn and shut the door behind me.

Downstairs, Patty is waiting for me on the sofa. Great. I'm in no mood for a speech. I pretend I don't see her.

"Listen, Mags, today's a new day. I smoothed things over best I could yesterday. Just stay away from that boy and everyone will forget about it, and we'll go back to normal."

"Why don't you like him? Just because he dresses a little differently?"

She rolls her eyes. "Well, yes. That's exactly why. And I guess you've heard him talk. He actually told Shelley she had gullyfluff on her sweater yesterday. What the hell was he talking about? Was that a weird word for boob?"

I'm sure the word is totally harmless. Probably was one of his "steampunkisms."

I look at my sister, the beautiful and popular one, and feel sad. Why is what everyone else thinks so important to Patty?

She flops back against the sofa cushion. "Anyway, enough about that boy. I'm really sorry about not taking what you told me more seriously. I was totally exhausted. If you're so stressed that you're seeing things, I should have been more helpful, but I've been stressed lately, too."

"What's wrong?" I'm being charitable, but inside I'm grumbling about what she said about Taj.

"The dance, Maggie. It's in two days! I hear Aiden is going to ask me today, but we need Ethan to ask you, then everything will be perfect." She reaches down and grabs her silver makeup bag. "Come here. Close your mouth."

"But—" I sit on the edge of the couch, not moving.

"Zip it." Patty is on me like a beauty ninja, coating my lips with plum-tinted lip gloss. "Don't know why you don't take the time to put on a little makeup in the morning," she says as she sweeps sparkling pink blush across my cheekbones and eyelids. "Just need a little mascara."

"You don't have to—"

Patty grabs a chunky tube of mascara from her makeup bag, shakes it, and pulls out a goo-covered wand. "Look up." She coats my strawberry-blond eyelashes black.

"But—"

"Remember how we always had matching haircuts? And braids? Remember when we were into French braids?"

I try to nod, but she brushes my hair so hard I can't manage it.

Finished, she stands back, puts her hands on her hips, and announces, "Gorgeous." She hands me a mirror.

I pause, remembering the scary reflection I saw in the mirror at Silver Lake, and the freaky lights floating behind my image in the mirror in our room.

Hesitantly, I peek at myself. "That's not me." She has managed to mask the raccoon eyes I've developed over the past week. My face actually sparkles.

Sunlight catches the glitter on Patty's face. "Of course it's you."

I look again. I guess it has to be me, but I feel like I'm in the wrong skin.

Patty pulls a vial out of her bag and gives herself a spritz. "Want?" she asks, directing the vial at me.

I shake my head. That reminds me. "Patty, have you ever heard of a perfume called Chanel Number Five?"

"Of course, it's from Paris. Been around for years. The designer is Coco Chanel. But it's mucho expensive." Patty claps her hands together and her eyes brighten. "Are you looking for a signature scent? Something for the dance? Here, try some of mine before you go right to the big-bucks stuff." She sprays a cloud of perfume in my direction.

This is the second clue pointing to Paris. "Thanks, Patty."

"No, problem. Now let's go. Today we're off to catch us some Wilson boys, sister." She grabs her backpack. Skipping out the door, she calls back, "Wear your navy peacoat, okay."

I don't answer. I run upstairs and grab the tweed coat from my room. I know Patty is ready to kill me, but too bad, I am still wearing it to school today. I need all the help I can get to solve the coat girl mystery so I can get back to finishing my painting for Peabody.

Before heading out the door, I turn and grab my sketchbook. My hand itches to draw.

No, more than that.

It *needs* to draw something.

Chapter Thirteen

Five days, twenty-three hours until the deadline.

I have to find Taj and tell him about the latest mysterious developments, but Patty is determined to keep me glued by her side today as she prowls the halls for the Wilson brothers. She gathers her silky hair behind her shoulders and creaks open the heavy school doors. "We're inside. Now ditch that ugly thing," she whispers while tugging on my coat.

I unbutton the soft velvet buttons, slip out of the sleeves, and fold it neatly over my arm. Feeling out of place all made up, I pull my hair forward to hide my face, and peer down the hall through a veil of red.

Patty pulls me close. "If we see Aiden and Ethan, try not to act too weird. Absolutely no ghost talk, got it?"

While my sister searches for the Wilson brothers, I search the crowded halls for a glimpse of Taj.

We walk a few more feet, and then Patty clutches my arm and yanks me toward her. "Theretheyare," she whispers so quickly it sounds like one word.

The huntress has found her quarry. Patty nearly pulls me off my feet as she hurries toward the two boys leaning on the wall outside of the cafeteria. They both wear faded jeans and black hoodies. Matching outfits. No wonder Patty likes them so much.

We approach and Patty slows down, putting a sexy swing in her hips. "Be cool, Maggie."

I stay behind her. She is in charge of this show.

"Hey, Patty," Aiden calls.

Patty stops, tosses her flaming-red mane behind her shoulders, and opens her green eyes wide. "Oh, Aiden. I didn't see you." She tilts her head and curls a lock of her shiny hair around her finger. "Hey, Ethan," she drawls.

Ethan nods in her direction. As Patty chats them up I stand by her side, uncomfortable and mute.

Then I see Taj weaving through the crowd. Today he sports a black fedora and a gray striped suit vest over a black tee. My heart leaps, then settles into a quick patter inside my chest.

Taj heads toward us and I make my escape, mumbling something about needing a notebook from my locker. I walk beside Taj and don't look back, although I can feel the heat of Patty's anger burning my back.

"You'll never believe what happened to me last night," I say as we turn the corner.

He glances down at me. "You fell into your sister's makeup bag?"

"Huh? Oh, yeah this." My hands flutter to my face. "Patty thought I needed a lift."

"You know you don't need it, right?"

My face warms and I stare at the floor. "Um, thanks."

We stop and stand under the stairwell to the second floor.

"So, what did you want to tell me?" he asks.

I look left, then right, to make sure we are alone. "Last night when I went to work on my painting, my hands started shaking like mad. Like they were possessed. But, the weird shakes only happen when I hold my paintbrush near the painting of the coat girl."

His eyebrows scrunch together. "That's odd."

"There's more. I—"

A crowd of kids pass by.

"I'll tell you later. Anyway, I have to find her. So, what am I gonna do? I have less than six days."

"Another séance?"

I shiver. "Um, maybe during library period we can figure out other, less creepy options."

"I won't be there today. Our English class is being dragged to the Ritz Theatre to see *The Taming of the Shrew*." He looks over my head and stares at something behind me. "I won't see you in art or library today."

"Oh, okay." I try to hide the disappointment in my voice.

"Don't worry, we'll figure this out."

He leads me toward the sign that has caught his attention—a big, glitter-covered poster advertising the Spring Fling.

"Um, Maggie. I was wondering—" He makes little circles on the floor with the toe of his brown leather boot.

My heart pounds so hard, I'm surprised my chest can contain it.

"I mean, I thought, you know, that maybe, if you weren't otherwise committed, you'd like to accompany me—" He looks up at the poster as if studying it intensely. "—to the Spring Fling Saturday night?"

"The dance?" Patty's face flashes in my mind, making my stomach tighten. "I'd love to." The second bell trills. I clap my hands together. "I can't wait." Then I take off up the stairs to my morning advisory class.

"Me, either," he calls after me.

In class, my insides twist in knots. Patty will freak. But on the other hand—I take a big gulp of air—a boy actually likes me!

I pull out my sketchbook and page through my nature sketches, dream notes, and drawings until I find a fresh sheet of paper. I bring my pencil down slowly. No trembles. I shake my head. Totally fine. Maybe my little talk got through to the coat girl.

Like a shooting star, my pencil flies across the pages. Chic women in long, flowing dresses, heads adorned with feathered and veiled hats, hands covered in elbow-length satin gloves. All morning I draw at a frantic pace, tuning out class after class, hopeful that when I get home I can get back to painting.

At the end of algebra class, I examine the sketches I drew while everybody else searched for common denominators. The drawings are different from my usual work. Silken gowns, and dresses flouncing with taffeta. Everything from ball gowns to slinky sheaths. Are these drawings mine?

I run to art class to show Ms. Cherry. She is sitting at her desk reading *American Artist* and drinking coffee, steam rising from the cup in a wavy circle.

I hand Ms. Cherry my sketchbook. Her eyes widen and her mouth drops open. She pulls off her glasses, wipes them on her sleeve, and puts them back on the edge of her nose. "These are beautiful, Maggie," she exclaims. "Do they have something to do with the mysterious entry that you have not shown me one bit of yet?"

"No, these are different." At least I hope they are different—as in, I actually drew them with no otherworldly influences.

"Amazing." She turns to a page containing a sketch of a woman with large, deep-set eyes and skinny, arching eyebrows, wearing a black fitted dress with a plunging neckline. "This one reminds me of Greta Garbo."

I scan my brain, trying to recall the name. "Did she sub for you when you had the flu?"

Ms. Cherry chuckles. "Sorry, I'm a bit of an old movie buff. Greta Garbo was an actress from the Forties."

She takes a large swig of coffee. "In fact, your drawings remind me of illustrations in a magazine called *Harpers Bazaar*. You should check them out."

During library study hall, I Google *Harpers Bazaar*, and Ms. Cherry is right. My drawings do look an awful lot like the ones in the old magazines. But what does it mean? Is the secret to identifying the ghost girl hidden in the pages of these old magazines? I search and search, but can find no connection, except that the images were drawn in the Forties and the coat's design is from the Forties. I wish Taj were here. Even if he couldn't figure out what the drawings meant, just being next to him would make me feel better.

All day, I continue to draw. My hands seem to be fine and my sketchbook fills quickly, but the drawings change. My first illustrations depicted beautiful women in gorgeous clothes. The new sketches are more like instructions on how to construct the clothes.

I jot down notes all over the pages—where to put in darts, hidden zippers, gathers, and seam allowances. Weird thing is, last year in consumer sciences class I was the biggest dweeb on Earth when it came to sewing. I could barely make a pillow that didn't look like a dog used it for a chew toy. Yet, sewing terms keep pouring onto the pages of my book. Where or who is this coming from?

I need to get to Silver Lake and see Miss Berk right away. I have this weird feeling that she knows more about the coat than she told me. And, if not, she knows about sewing. Maybe she can give me some answers.

CHAPTER FOURTEEN

Five days, fifteen hours until the deadline.

When I reach Silver Lake, the front porch is loaded with cardboard boxes. A new resident must be moving in. From somewhere upstairs, Suzi sings a jazzy rendition of "Memories" from the musical *Cats* in her high soprano voice. Boy, she can really belt out a song. She should try out for her school's senior musical. I navigate through the stacked boxes. After I talk to Miss Berk, I'll give Mrs. Valentine and Suzi a hand situating the new guest.

I want to catch Miss Berk alone, but with the residents already set up in the craft room for watercolor painting, I don't have time. I know how much they look forward to painting with me.

After making sure everyone has a set of paints, brushes, paper, and a bowl of fresh water, I slide into a chair next to Miss Berk, my sketchbook on my lap. I am planning to ask her about my sketches when we take a break, but right now my hand itches to dip my brush into a well of indigo paint.

My brush flies across the page with sweeping, confident strokes. It is as if my hand is possessed—but in a good way. I paint a picture of a sketch I did earlier of a graceful, blonde woman wearing a long white dress belted with a black sash and a flouncy flower on the top of the bodice. I manage to render it even more realistically with the addition of color.

Next to me, Miss Berk works on a painting of a smoky gray kitten with emerald eyes. "Remember Minka, my kitty, Freyda?"

I read that Alzheimer's patients often can remember the distant past better than recent events. "She looks very pretty," I say, and wonder if she'll be able to decipher the sewing terms in my sketches in her altered state.

"What are you painting, dear?" She glances at my painting and freezes. With a strangled cry she drops her brush, spraying her painting with green pigment, and shuffles out of the room.

I drop my own brush and follow her into the parlor, where she is slumped on the couch with her head down and hands covering her face. "What's wrong? What happened?" I try to keep my voice relaxed.

"Why were you painting that, Maggie?" She looks up, tears streaming down her wrinkled cheeks. "How did you know? I never t—" Her voice catches and she starts sobbing. Her watery eyes search mine, pleading.

Miss Berk is in the present now. She called me Maggie, but I've never seen her get upset like this. What is so disturbing about my painting?

Mrs. Valentine finds us in the parlor, and rushes to Miss Berk's side. "You poor dear, take a deep breath and relax." She turns to me. "Poor thing has been eating next to nothing these days."

"Is she sick?"

"She's just tired." She pats Miss Berk's hand. "I'm going to get you some soup, dear."

My hand goes to my birthmark; it itches like the bites of a thousand mosquitoes.

Suzi flies down the stairs, coffee sloshing over the edges of her cup. "What's going on?"

I lean my head back against the sofa and open my mouth to answer, but the smell of chicken soup drifts in from the kitchen and my mind twists toward another time. The parlor disappears and I find myself in a different place.

I hold a crust of dried bread in one hand and a tin bowl of gray soup in the other. My lips touch the metal bowl and I drink the horrible-tasting liquid, following it with the tasteless bread. I want more, but know there will be no more until tomorrow. My insides are burning. I can't believe I've kept down the awful meal. Far away, I hear a voice.

"Maggie. Maggie." Mrs. Valentine shakes my shoulder. "Thought I'd lost you, too."

"Huh?" I blink; my hands tremble like crazy. Before I can spit out what I saw, the memory slips away like smoke through my fingers.

Mrs. Valentine holds her hand out to Miss Berk, who takes it and stands shakily. "Why don't you call it a night, child," Mrs. Valentine says. "I'll see to it that Gittel is settled in her room."

"Who?" *Did she just say what I thought she said?*

"Oh, I'm sorry. I guess you never called her by her first name. You're so polite. Miss Berk's first name is Gittel."

The coat girl's Gittel?

"Wait, Gittel—" I reach for her, but she shrinks away from me and cries even harder.

"She needs to rest, child." Mrs. Valentine moves between me and Miss Berk. "You can talk to her tomorrow. Right now I need to get her to bed."

They disappear into the elevator, and my answers ride up and away with them.

Suzi pats me on the shoulder. "You okay, girlfriend?"

"I need to talk to Miss Berk."

She plops down on the sofa, sets her coffee on the table, and rests her chin in her hands. "Knew old lady Berk was an odd bird, but what the heck just happened?"

"That's what I have to find out."

"You can't get yourself all worked up over this thing. She's only operating with half a jar of marbles, and most of them are rolling away fast."

"Yeah, I know." I sigh. "So, need any help moving the new person in?"

"What new person?"

"Saw the boxes out front, figured—"

"Oh, that's more junk to take over to Salvation Army Thrift."

Salvation Army Thrift? Mrs. Valentine talked about spring cleaning. Clearing her attic of the residents' things. Duh. Now it makes sense. "Suzi, when you were helping to box up the stuff, did you happen to notice an old tweed coat with a black fur collar?"

"Sure did. Tried it on, but I was too much woman for it." She puts her hands under her boobs and pushes them up. "See?" She giggles. "What about it?"

I look around, unsure.

"Come on. I know we only see each other once in a while. But you can trust me," Suzi says, her face serious.

"You have time for a story?" I ask.

During the bike ride home, my mind spins as fast as the spokes on my wheels. Is Gittel okay? If she is my ghost's Gittel, I am super-close to finding the coat girl. I told Suzi everything that had happened since I bought the tweed coat, and even though I'm not sure she believed me, she is willing to help. She said she'll try to pump her grandmother for information about Miss Berk's past.

I pop a wheelie. But as the front tire lifts off the ground, the back one spins out on some wet leaves. I skid and crash to the ground. When I stand and inspect myself, I find a skinned knee to add to all the injuries I got this past week. Yep, I'm still as graceful as a hippo on rollerblades.

I brush myself off and ignore the blood seeping through my jeans.

I'm positive Miss Berk recognized the dress I drew. But why did it upset her so much?

I hope when I get the answers, I'll be able to paint again. I have to!

At home I walk in on the tail end of Mom's phone conversation. "Thank you, Tori. Let me know as soon as you get word."

Mom sees me and lowers her voice, turning her back. I pretend I don't hear anything and pour myself a glass of cold milk.

After she hangs up the phone, Mom turns to me, her face pinched. "Let's sit down in the livin' room and talk."

I gulp. Could she know about the séance? I never even told Patty about it. Or is it something else? Is she seeing things in me, things I don't even realize, that are reminding her of Bridget before she . . .

"Patty," she calls. "Come downstairs for a wee minute."

Patty runs down the steps and joins us. Mom sinks down on the sofa and pats the two cushions next to her. Puffs of dust sparkle in the sunlight. I study it, wondering how I would replicate the effect in paint.

Patty sits next to Mom.

"Come here, Margaret," Mom says.

Mom only calls me by my full name when things are really serious. I sit next to her, the milk I just drank curdling in my stomach.

"I heard from the realtor today. We have a lad who is very interested in seein' the house."

I bite the inside of my cheek and pick at my fingernails. "Do you think he'll buy it?"

Losing our house will be horrible. First Dad, then his house.

"I know it's been hard on you wee ones, what with me working so much." She lets out a ragged breath. "If I could change things I would, love. I love this house—" Her voice breaks.

"We'll be okay," I say.

Mom makes a small, strangled noise. "We will be, darlin', we will be. I feel yer father lookin' down on us. Watchin' over us."

"Are we still moving to the Willowdale Apartments if we sell the house, Mom?" Patty asks.

"That's the plan," Mom replies.

"They have a pool, Mags. Think of the cute bikinis we can rock this summer."

Like I really care about rocking a bikini. This is our home. The one we shared with Dad.

"Nothing's definite. Just wanted to let you girls know." Mom pats my leg. "Think of it as a new adventure."

I groan inside and glance at Patty. She's smiling. How can she be smiling?

In the hall I run my hand over the wall where our heights have been recorded over the years. Patty's consistent one-inch lead has always bugged me. I study the writing next to each line, Dad's writing. The new owners will probably paint over the marks and erase the history of our childhood. Sadness splinters my body, threatening to crack it open like an eggshell.

I grab the tweed coat, inhale deeply, and close my eyes, letting myself drift away.

With the coat on, I enter Dad's studio, pick up my brush, and dip it in a dash of umber paint. But instead of touching it to the canvas, I am propelled toward the wall. My hand splats my loaded paintbrush onto the wall and starts moving. I am writing. No, I am not writing. My hand is. I can't control it. I try to pull back, but can't.

The sweat rolling down my temple feels like a spider skittering down my face. My birthmark burns. With all my might, I try to reclaim my arm. Pulling, pulling . . .

The connection breaks. The brush clatters to the floor and I fall back, landing on my butt. I wiggle my fingers. They move. Mine.

I raise my eyes. The words "TELL GITTEL" are slashed across the wall in dark umber paint.

I lurch to my feet and run out of the room, slamming the door behind me.

Back in my room, I pull out my sketchbook and draw until my hand cramps. I don't mind the pain. I'm grateful I can feel it. At least I know it's mine.

Even in my hopeless state, my hand continues sketching garments.

I have to find her. These sketches must hold clues. I need to figure them out.

As I draw, I stew over the fiasco with the Wilson boys and the thrill of Taj asking me to the dance. Patty avoided me all day because I left Ethan Wilson to talk with Taj. If she can't accept who I am and the people I choose to be friends with, then . . .

The steps squeak as she comes upstairs. She stops in the doorway, but I don't look up. I don't have to. Her anger burns my skin like a fire.

Remember, even your own can turn on you, a ghostly voice whispers inside my head. The image of a stern woman in a gray smock flickers in my mind for an instant.

Our room is thick with silence as Patty prepares for bed. I turn away from her and busy myself with sketching.

Finally, she says, "Why do you hate me?"

I raise my eyes from my sketchbook. "I don't hate you, Patty."

"I want things to go back to the way they used to be, Mags. I miss my sister."

"You're the one always telling me to stop living in the past."

"You didn't die, Maggie."

No, I am living my own life. The way I want. "I don't know if I can ever be the way I used to be. You're going to have to accept me the way I am."

She sighs. "Okay, okay. You win."

But I can see in her eyes that she's not giving up. Patty is used to me doing everything she tells me to do.

She stares over my shoulder and whispers, "Whatcha drawing?"

I hand over my sketchbook.

"Wow, Maggie, your book's almost full." Her eyes brighten as she examines my drawings. "The shading is like, perfect. They look like real people. Really, this is good. You should enter one of these in that art contest."

"I might have to." Not that some little sketch has any kind of chance.

Patty turns and pulls something off the bookshelf. "Here." She hands me her unused sketchbook. Dad gave us both sketchbooks, hoping art might be something the three of us could share. "You might as well use it. I never will. Think of it as a peace offering."

I open the book and an electric thrill skitters from the crown of my head to the soles of my feet. Pages and pages of clean, white paper.

"So, about today with the Wilson boys—" I begin.

"They are so cute." Patty stretches out on her bed. "I just know Ethan would like you if you gave him a chance. Can't you try being normal? Like before you brought that stupid coat into the house?"

"I am normal." Does she think something more is wrong with me?

"Great. So it's agreed. Can I tell Sugar you'll stop hanging out with that weird boy now and we'll get back to work on Ethan."

"What? No. How can you keep asking me that? I thought you understood." I hug my pillow tighter.

"Why?" She punches her own pillow and draws in a loud, shuddering breath. "Please, Mags. Sugar doesn't want to be seen with you. I covered for you today with Ethan, said you had to borrow math notes from that dork, but I can't keep doing it." She leans forward and narrows her eyes. "It's us or him, Maggie."

"I thought it was me and you, Patty."

"It is. But we need friends, too." She sighs. "The girls are talking crap about you. As if you would ever go out with that boy." She is quiet for a moment. "You aren't, are you?"

I stay silent, simmering.

"Well?"

I harden my voice. "The girls never really liked me anyway. They just tolerated me because I'm your sister. You think I don't know that? Anyway, I'm fine with Taj being my friend. He doesn't care what coat I wear or what I do. And what if I do want to go out with him?"

"How can you say that? Of course they like you. Or they would if you tried to get to know them better. Come to Sugar's house when she invites us for movie night. Stop always making excuses not to hang out."

"But, I don't like the same things they do," I explain. "Taj is an artist like me—"

"Let me put it bluntly. You are who you associate with in school. I've worked really hard to get us in with the popular kids. If we move into Willowdale it's just going to get tougher." Patty sighs. "We'll be apartment kids. Can't even afford our own house. We might have to start all over."

"I thought you liked the idea. The pool and all—"

"I was just trying to make Mom feel better."

"Well, I don't care about being popular anyway."

"Are you crazy?" Patty asks. "Let me rephrase that. Are you even crazier than you appear?"

"What do you mean by that? What are you implying?"

"Forget it."

"Taj is nice and he cares about me."

"Bet you didn't know his dad is a mortician and he actually lives above the funeral home. Sugar told me that he may even sleep in the same room as cadavers!"

"Don't be ridiculous, Patty. Their apartment is separate from the funeral home section. Of course, Sugar would say something stupid like that. You're just proving my point."

Patty places her index finger on her chin. "Wait. He lives in the last place we saw Dad. You know, at the viewing. Is that what this is all about?"

"What do you mean?"

"Latching on to him because he has some kind of weird association with Dad."

I slap my sketchbook shut and slam it on the floor. "That's totally stupid! I can't believe you'd even suggest that."

"Well—"

"He's my friend. And he's important to me."

"Guess he's more important than I am," Patty says. She pops in her earbuds and turns her back.

"And I'm going to the Spring Fling with him," I whisper. "Love you much, Patty," I grumble, louder so she can hear me over her music. No answer. The only sound is the rattle of the radiator.

I close my eyes.

I am in a vast, chilly warehouse. Silverware, musical instruments, hats, shoes, and clothing are strewn about, and there is an odd jumble of scents in the air—cologne, sweat, mothballs. I turn to my left and see the coat girl picking through a pile of dresses. "We need to sort these by color," she says.

We dig through cotton, silk, and satin dresses and put them in their proper piles. Stacks of green, blue, brown, and black clothing surround us.

"Why won't you let me paint?" I ask.

She doesn't look at me. "You will when you find Gittel."

"I think I've found Gittel."

"Good, then you are getting close to knowing."

"Knowing what? Why won't you tell me your name?" I ask.

"Ask Gittel."

"Why?"

She doesn't answer.

"Then I need more clues."

She stays silent, searching through the mountains of clothing.

"Where are we?"

"Canada." She tosses aside a green cardigan.

"The country? Are you French Canadian?"

She shakes her head. "I thought I'd start with this one," she says, pointing to something in a notebook she pulled out of her pocket. "This dress won't be easy."

She traces her fingers over the lines of a sketch I recognize from my sketchbook drawings. How the heck—

"She wanted this gown made from blue silk. Silk is very hard to work with." She looks up and smiles. "It's as slippery as a fish."

"Who is she?"

"She's the Monster's wife. Let's not speak of her," she whispers.

The Monster? How has the coat girl gotten my sketches?

I pick up a teal dress by its sleeve. The coat girl shakes her head, so I drop it and keep hunting.

"Please tell me your name," I say, giving her a sideways glance. "I might not be able to help you without it."

"Remember everything I say. You're getting close to knowing," she answers.

"I am?"

"Now hurry. We won't make the deadline. We must finish two dresses by Saturday, twelve sharp."

I turn around and find myself in a different building, where I am seated in a dusty attic, coughing. Folded clothing is stacked high against one wall, and a pair of old-fashioned black sewing machines hum as the coat girl and another young girl pump the cast iron treadles. I realize this is the same girl I'd seen when we were hiding behind the bushes from the bad men, but she is much thinner and sickly looking. It is Gittel. Sunlight filters through small windows, sending pale shafts of light across the floor's rough oak planking. The coat girl hunches over her machine, feeding blue fabric under the foot.

"Gittel. Gittel Berk?" I ask.

She doesn't answer, but concentrates on making dress patterns out of thin tissue, her hands moving lightning-fast over the flimsy paper. Something about the way Gittel moves reminds me of Miss Berk. Are they truly the same person? I want to grab her arm and ask again if she is Gittel Berk but I sense I should leave her alone.

Above me, exposed rafters crisscross under a pointed roof. I look out one of the narrow windows and see a beautiful garden filled with pink and yellow roses. In the distance, smoke stacks send wisps of gray into the azure sky. A deep sadness penetrates my bones. What is it? Why can't I remember what is causing this sorrow?

When I turn back, the coat girl twirls a shimmering blue gown on a dressmaker's form. The bottom of the gown falls into a pool of ruffles on the dusty floor.

"She will be pleased," flashes in my mind. Who is "she"? Her identity floats around the edges of my memory.

I am startled by footsteps on the stairs, they are getting closer. Click. Click. Click.

The coat girl glances over at Gittel and a look of fear registers in both their eyes.

I rush to their side and we huddle together, trembling. A dark shadow grows on the wall, and in steps a grim-looking woman.

"It's Frau Hoess," the coat girl whispers.

The woman approaches the dress hanging on the form and examines every stitch. "Flawless, simply flawless," she says in an astonished voice. "Such a clever girl for a—"

A heavy weight falls on my chest.

CHAPTER SIXTEEN

Four days, twenty-three hours until the deadline.

I open my eyes and find Seurat on top of me, kneading his paws into my ribs. I push him off gently and write "Frau Hoess" in my sketchbook before the name escapes me.

Such a clever girl for a . . . a what? I've heard a phrase like that before, but when? The words flutter away like a plastic bag in the wind.

Get it done fast. Deadline. Deadline. The desperate demand echoes strangely in my ears as I pull on a pair of jeans, a sweater, and the tweed coat. My thoughts churn. *Must be finished with another dress by Saturday, twelve sharp.* It's like catching a glimpse of something floating in a swirl of water just before it's sucked down a drain.

I'm late for school, but it's a shortened day, the start of spring break, so hopefully the teachers didn't take attendance. My sneakers squeak as I run down the hall. Rounding a corner, I almost smash into our principal, Mr. Sanders. "Slow down there, missy. Do you have a hall pass?"

I shake my head. I need to think fast. "Girl problems?" I've never used that excuse, but Patty told me it always worked for her.

He huffs. "I'll let you go this time, but next time you better have a pass. Hurry down to the auditorium. They're showing a movie."

Yes. A small victory.

I open the heavy auditorium doors just wide enough to squeeze through, and lower myself into an empty seat in the back. I watch the movie on the big screen, half-distracted by my latest vision, when I am startled to hear the words, "Frau Hoess" spoken by one of the actors. I sit up straighter and nudge the girl next to me. "What's this movie called?"

"*The Boy in the Striped Pajamas*," she whispers. "They told us we have to write a stupid one-page paper about it. Due first day after break. It really blows."

The two boys in the movie were friends in a place where labels such as religion and race meant life or death. But they didn't care about such distinctions. They liked each other for the people they were inside. But tragically, one boy was the son of a Nazi official and the other boy was imprisoned at Auschwitz.

The bell rings and we thunder out of the auditorium. Sunglasses are suddenly all the rage. Nobody likes to be seen with red, puffy eyes.

I wait for Taj by his locker. He strides toward me, grinning. "Guess what?"

"What?"

"I put the finishing touches on my sculpture last night. Want to see it?"

I grin back. "Of course." I lean in closer. "Guess who I found yesterday? At least I think I did."

"No." Taj's eyes go wide.

"Yep. Gittel."

"Details, m'lady."

I grab his arm. "And there's more."

"More?"

I can barely hear him over the din of clanging lockers and excited voices.

"Can I tempt you with a gastronomical treat?" he asks.

"Huh?"

"Want to go to lunch?"

I skipped breakfast this morning, but lately worry has a way of filling me, tricking my appetite. "I have to let Patty know, or . . . oh, the heck with it. Sure, sounds great."

I hesitate outside Vito's Pizza. This is a popular hangout and is probably filled with kids from our school, including Patty and the girls.

Taj continues walking. "Care for something a little more adventurous?"

"Absolutely." It's as if he can read my mind.

Taj leads me down a side street to a tiny restaurant called Marrakesh tucked between a Starbucks and a CVS. Inside, I lean back in a cushioned chair in front of a low, round table covered with filmy fabric. A gold tray tops the table, and candles flicker on oval sconces that resemble medieval torches. Dancing candlelight dapples the burgundy-and-gold gauze drapes. So many colors and textures. Dad would have loved this place.

Taj orders for us. Moments later our waiter returns with a tray full of bowls heaped with food. Taj passes me a small plate, and then points to a creamy, golden dip swirled with orange-colored spice that reminds me of a sunset over desert dunes.

"This is hummus. It's made from chickpeas. And this," he points to a green-speckled dip, "is baba ganoush. It's made from eggplant. There's also some rice and grilled lamb."

"It's kind of spicy, but I think I like it." The dip is smooth and creamy with just a hint of peppery burn.

"Garlic and paprika gives it a kick," Taj says.

In between bites, I fill Taj in on Miss Berk and her weird reaction to my sketches. "So get this. Miss Berk's first name is Gittel."

"*The* Gittel?"

"I think so, but there's more. It's kind of hard to believe, but last night I had another dream. In this dream, I was given the name of a person. A bad person. I heard the name again in the movie at school." I hesitate, not wanting to utter the name. "Frau Hoess."

Taj's eyes open wide and he splays his long fingers out on the tabletop. "Hoess, as in Auschwitz Commandant Hoess from the movie?"

"Exactly." I clasp my hands together, my knuckles turning white as I take a deep breath. "I think Gittel and the coat girl were prisoners in that concentration camp."

The portrait of the desperate girl wearing the tweed coat flashes in my mind. This time I clearly see the yellow Star of David patch sewn on the left lapel. The room shifts, and a wave of dizziness washes over me. The pita bread sinks like a rock in my stomach.

Taj leans forward, his knees touching mine. "Maybe you can help her, Maggie. After all these years, you can discover who she was and let her know she mattered. Maybe she'll finally have some peace."

"But why me? I mean, I know it sounds ridiculous, but I truly believe the coat called to me."

"Maybe you're sensitive to that kind of thing. We artists are known for being sensitive people."

"But why not you? You were there at the thrift shop on the same day. You are creating art about genocide. You would have been the better choice."

"She felt a connection to you. After all, you know Gittel."

"True." I scratch my head. "You said she wants to know she mattered. So even after you die, your spirit, or ghost or whatever, still cares whether people think about you?" Like caring whether your seat at the dinner table was taken away or your family sells the house that meant so much to you?

Or maybe something else. Something more.

After lunch, Taj and I race over to Silver Lake, pictures from the movie replaying in my head. I am determined to find out what Miss Berk knows about the coat girl, but it's going to be tricky. I don't want to upset her again. And I can't bear to make her cry. I can't imagine being held in Auschwitz, and I can't blame her if she doesn't want to ever speak about that terrible place again.

When we arrive, we decide Taj will wait on the front step while I speak to Miss Berk. I stare at the front door, wringing my hands. *What will I say? How will I start?*

Taj pats my shoulder. "It'll be okay," he whispers.

Inside, I find Mrs. Valentine in her office flipping through a big pile of mail. She looks up, and I see the hint of a shadow pass over her eyes.

"Hi, just came in to check on Miss Berk. Did she get over her last spell?" I nibble on my nails, then stop myself.

"I meant to call you, Maggie, but as you can see I'm up to my elbows in paperwork. I know how much you care for Miss Berk. Unfortunately, she took a turn for the worse. She was admitted to the hospital last night."

My heart skips a beat and my mouth goes dry. "Hospital? Will she be okay?" *Did I do this to her?*

"She's been very sick for quite a while, dear. Her ticker is slowing down." She sighs. "We all wind down eventually."

The news is a punch to the stomach. She has to be all right. She just has to. She holds all the answers.

Suzi slides into the room and grabs my arm. "Come here, girlfriend." She pulls me into the parlor.

"Mrs. Berk's in the hospital," I say

She rubs my arm. "Don't worry, she's a tough old bird."

"Did you find anything out about her past?"

"Nada. Grams knows nothing." She pulls back the front window curtain and peeks outside.

"Hey, who's the hottie out front?"

"My friend, Taj."

"Suzi!" Mrs. Valentine calls.

"Coming." She winks at me. "Methinks he's more than a friend." She giggles and runs off.

On my way through the foyer, I catch the scent of Miss Berk's perfume and turn, expecting to see her. But the room is empty. What if she never comes back? What if she dies?

I close the front door of Silver Lake and sit on the steps next to Taj. When he sees my face, I don't have to say a word. He puts his arm around me.

Coat in hand, I've barely walked through the front door before Patty starts in on me. "Where'd you go?" She sniffs the air. "Your breath reeks."

I cup my hand over my nose and mouth and breathe in. Okay, it is pretty garlicky. "I ate at a Middle Eastern restaurant with Taj."

Anger turns her face stony. "I saved a seat for you at Vito's."

"Sorry." But they never even asked me to join them. "And whether you like it or not, he is my friend." I stomp by her and up the stairs. "And not for any weird psycho-babble reasons," I call down.

In my room, I Google "Hoess" and find out the family lived just outside the Auschwitz prison. There was some truth to the movie I watched earlier at school. But their real first names were Rudolph and Hedwig, not Ralph and Elsa like in the movie.

I have to tell the coat girl what I've discovered. Perhaps just me knowing what she went through will be enough to let her rest in peace.

When I open the door to Dad's studio, the coat girl's image stares back at me from the easel. I slip into the tweed coat and approach her. "You were held captive by Hedwig Hoess at Auschwitz. Am I right?"

Her eyes look so sad that I reach toward her. The lights flicker, and then the room goes pitch-black. The tiny hairs on the back of my neck bristle. I turn, my arms stretched out in front of me. Insects buzz in my ear and I spin, swatting at them.

The stink of rotting flesh fills the room. My hand flies to my face, covering my nose and mouth. I gag. Bile rises in my throat, but I manage to swallow it down.

Cries—mournful, hopeless sounds—surround me. Hands grab at my legs, fingers tug on the hem of my shirt. I slap them away and shuffle backward until I slam into the wall. My heart pounds in my chest.

Growls. Snapping jaws. Sharp, deep barks. Out of the blackness, German shepherds with huge teeth creep toward me and their cold eyes bore into me. They inch closer, surrounding me, and I have nowhere to run. Their warm saliva slides down my arms, their hot breath blows on my fingers.

"Stop!"

The lights snap back on. The room goes silent; my arms are dry and cool. My eyes still dart about, thinking that any minute one of those vicious dogs will materialize and lunge at me. I take off, not even bothering to shut the door.

CHAPTER SEVENTEEN

Four days, eleven hours until the deadline.

The dark sky sends violet shadows across our bedroom. Pale moonlight spills silver across the floor.

The light shines on an unfinished dress in the center of the slant-walled room. I sit on a hard wooden chair in front of the ancient sewing machine. My fingers draw a fine thread through the needle's tiny hole. Swaths of white chiffon cover my lap. My hands are rough on the delicate fabric, and I am afraid my ragged cuticles might snag it.

I look around, but the coat girl is nowhere to be seen, and young Gittel bends over a bucket, retching. I look down. I am dressed in a striped, raggedy dress. I don't know what to do. I want to help Gittel, but I know there is no time.

I twist my head to look at a clock hanging over the doorway. Ten minutes after eleven! Less than an hour to finish, I think to myself.

Huh? Me finish?

I sew and sew, every so often glancing back, looking from Gittel's sick body to the clock's hands.

I examine the sketch of the dress I am making. It is familiar, since I'd drawn it only the day before and painted it in watercolor at Silver Lake. A pleated, white chiffon dress cinched at the waist with black silk tied in a bow. A black flower fashioned out of the same silk fabric will adorn the bust line.

Ten minutes before twelve, and I still haven't attached the sash or the flower. I worry about Gittel, pale as ice curled on the floor, but know I can't help her until I've finished.

Somehow I sew like a pro, and the dress looks gorgeous, if I can just get the finishing touches done in time. I pin everything in place.

Five minutes before twelve. "Don't worry, Gittel. It'll be okay."

The silk accessories need to be hand-sewn, and that takes time. The stitches have to be neat and uniform. They are very particular. They?

Sewing.

Four minutes before twelve.

Finished the sash.

Two minutes before twelve.

Only two minutes left for the flower. I'll never make it. Sweat rolls down my back and my fingers move swiftly despite throbbing pain. Where is the coat girl?

One minute before twelve. Still time. Sixty seconds. "Almost done, Gittel."

Sewing. Sewing.

A door slams downstairs. Footsteps ascend the steps. Gittel sobs quietly. I catch her eye and she mouths, "I'm sorry."

The woman stands in front of me, her mouth in a tight line.

Five minutes and fifteen seconds after twelve.

I pull the last stitch, tie off the thread, and look up. The woman stares at me. Proudly, I hang my new creation on the dress form next to the blue silk dress.

SMACK!

Pinpricks of pain flash across my back, and I drop to my knees. Two more sharp blows follow.

I spring from my bed, run into the bathroom, and slam the door. I pull up my nightgown, and with my back to the mirror, twist my neck to look over my shoulder. What I see makes the blood drain from my face. Three angry welts crisscross the area between my shoulder blades.

My hand trembles as I touch the spots. I clench my teeth and wince. Pinpricks of blood rise from the slashes. But it was just a dream, how—

A shiver shakes my body and I sink to the floor. A quick rap on the door makes me jump.

"You almost done in there?" Patty shouts.

"Just a minute." I dab the blood on my back with a paper towel and toss it in the trashcan. When I open the door Patty shoves past me. "Hurry up. Gotta pee." She slams the door shut.

Alone in the hall, I stare at the studio door, shut since the horror show of last night. I imagine the coat girl striding out, pointing at me.

My stomach flips, and I think I might throw up.

I have to talk to Gittel. And soon.

After I dress, I call Silver Lake and find out Miss Berk is still in intensive care. She has to get better. I have to talk to her. I might never be able to paint again—or worse.

After Googling Hedwig Hoess and taking more notes, I call Taj, and we decide to meet in the park before heading to Brandonville Town Library to do some intensive research. I wonder what he'll say about the lashes etched on my back.

The sun shines bright on this Saturday, and the park fills with people eager to leave their stuffy houses and feel its warmth on their faces. I meet Taj behind the playground and tell him about my dream, barely pausing to take a breath, not wanting to forget any details. "In my dream I knew I had to make two dresses by a twelve o'clock deadline, so I sewed and sewed—but I didn't make it. Then this happened and I woke up." I turn my back into the shadow of a large pine tree so the whole world doesn't see. Wincing when the fabric grazes the cuts, I pull up my sweater high enough to show the slashes crisscrossing my back.

"Jeez, I can't believe . . . but I do." Taj brings his finger to my skin and lightly touches one of the angry welts. "Youch. Does it hurt very badly?"

My body melts with his touch. "Just when I move." I let my sweater fall back down and turn to face him. "She wants me to find Gittel, and I don't think she's going to stop until I do." He holds out both hands and I take them. "Until Miss Berk gets released from the hospital, we have to find out more about Hedwig Hoess."

Hand in hand, we walk to the Brandonville Town Library, passing tall oak trees that are just beginning to form bright green buds. Tulips tilt their scarlet blossoms toward the sky. My mind instinctually mixes cadmium with a touch of ultramarine blue for the flowers' deep red color.

I lean closer to Taj. "Thanks. Thanks for believing me."

He squeezes my hand.

I head toward the bank of computers, but Taj pulls me back. "I've been searching the Internet all night for info. Let's go old-school and crack open some books."

After finding the call numbers for books on the Holocaust, we wander down the aisles and I breathe in the musty smells of old books and ink. I find a book simply titled *Auschwitz* and pull it from the shelf. We settle down together in a corner, a stack of books in front of us. I try to get comfortable, but my back throbs. I snuggle next to Taj's side and we open the books one by one.

Photographs litter the pages. Mass graves heaped with bodies, limbs strewn every which way; children clinging to their mothers' legs and crying as they are prodded toward a smoking crematorium; bags of human hair waiting for transport to become stuffing for bedding; and lampshades gruesomely constructed of stretched human skin. I try to keep down my breakfast. We saw pictures when we studied the Holocaust in seventh grade, but none as graphic as these.

Why did anyone want to record this gruesome event? How sick did these human minds become? Windowless train cars crowded with bodies. People turned to skin and bones. And there are photos of SS members partying it up. Feasting. Dancing. Singing. My stomach can't stop churning. I can't stop picturing the coat girl and young Gittel.

Taj taps my knee. "This is interesting." He reads from the book he holds.

"'After transport, the Jews were told to relinquish all their personal items. These items were stored in warehouses the SS called Canada'."

"Canada. Like in my dream. But why Canada?"

Taj skims over the text. "It says they believed Canada was the land of abundance." He turns a page. "Over the years, people have found many of these items in antique and curio shops."

"And thrift shops."

"Precisely."

I go back to the book I was skimming and turn another page, then flip back—a photograph stops me. It shows a party, tables loaded with food and wine, men and women laughing and dancing, swastikas decorating the men's lapels. In the background, very small but still visible, a woman stands on a stage. She wears a white chiffon dress with a black silk sash and flower! The very dress I dreamed about making last night. The same exact dress I drew that freaked out Miss Berk.

My body goes numb and the book slides from my hands. The thud echoes like a thunderclap in the quiet of the library.

"What's wrong?" Taj retrieves the fallen book and opens it.

"Page fifty-six. See the woman in white? She's wearing the dress I made in my dream. The one I didn't finish in time." I reach my hand behind my back and cringe when my fingers find the cuts. "The one I got whipped for." Taj reads the caption: Hedwig Hoess holds dinner party for SS compatriots.

My voice trembles. "I have to get out of here." I can barely breathe.

Heads turn as I sprint between the aisles of bookshelves and out the door. Once outside, I can't stop. Stumbling down the path behind the library, I enter the woods surrounding Hopkin's Pond. The trail narrows, and sharp thorns catch on my sweater, pricking me. I fall twice, skinning the palms of my hands. When I reach the pond, I stop and bend over to catch my breath.

Footsteps sound behind me. Taj stops, huffing and puffing. "Why'd you run from me?"

"Had to get out. Couldn't breathe. Had to escape."

"Let's sit." He takes a deep breath. "I think a bit of ruminating is in order."

We sit side by side on a big, flat rock. For a few moments we stare at the pond, not talking. A mallard duck lands in front of us. It dips its emerald-feathered head under the surface, and then brings it up, shaking droplets of water into the air that sparkle like loose diamonds.

"Taj, you'll be honest with me if I ask you a question, right?"

"Always."

I pick up a handful of smooth stones and toss them in the water one by one. The ripples widen, then disappear. "Do you think this could all be in my head? I mean, I could have heard the name Hoess when we studied the Holocaust at school. Maybe there is no ghost. Maybe something's wrong with me. I mean really wrong."

"Honestly? It is a possibility." He pauses for a beat. "But the evidence for a haunting is quite compelling." He skips a rock over the water with a flick of his wrist. It bounces five times. "For example, how do you explain the dress? You drew it, dreamed about it, and now we've discovered it actually exists."

Dark clouds roll in, blackening the sky. "So you believe there is a ghost?" In the distance, thunder rumbles. "Then let me ask you this." I swallow past a huge lump growing in my throat. Will I really say it out loud? This thought is mine, always locked and closely guarded. If I let it out, will it be the beginning of the end? Will my feelings and emotions drain away from me like water through a sieve, floating away just like Dad?

"What did you want to ask me?" Taj asks in a soft voice.

I clear my throat. "My Dad died three years ago," I say quietly. "Why didn't *his* ghost come to me?"

Gently, Taj bumps his foot against mine. "I'm sorry about your dad, Maggie." He tosses another pebble. "Maybe it's a good thing. Maybe he's in a good place, not tortured like the coat girl's ghost."

"I never got to say goodbye," I say in a small voice. "He died in his room, all alone."

My eyes fill. I should stop talking. I won't be able to hold it together. But the brakes on my mouth refuse to work. "I wonder if he was scared. What if his ghost is out there but he just doesn't want to talk to me? What if he's mad at me?" I turn my head and wipe my eyes.

"With my father being an undertaker, I've grown up surrounded by death." Taj skips another rock across the water. "I never told anyone what I'm about to tell you."

He grabs more stones and rattles them in his hand. "One day I went with my father to the hospital to pick up a body—" He stops and takes a deep breath.

"And?"

He clears his throat. "Anyway, I was sitting in the hall bouncing a super ball against the wall, waiting." He rubs the handful of stones together in his fist and they crunch against each other. "The ball rolled into a room. I went to get it and found it under a chair. When I stood up, I noticed the woman in the bed. She made the creepiest noise I'd ever heard. Scared the heck out of me. I yelled out for my father, but before he reached me, the woman died."

"How did you know she died?"

"The sound. She took in a huge breath. This eerie gasping, whistling noise rose from her throat. That was it. She never exhaled."

"At least she wasn't alone."

"I don't think she even knew I was there, but I still have horrible nightmares about it." He drops the stones and takes my hand. "I think your dad waited for you to be out of the room. Perhaps he spared you."

My dad spared me?

"My father says it's common for a terminal patient to hang on until they are alone. Maybe death needs to be a private thing for some people."

Clouds drift across the sun and the air grows colder. The woods darken. I shiver and Taj pulls me close and puts his arm around my shoulder. The emptiness I expected to feel after letting go of my secret does not come. Instead I feel a sort of lightness after sharing with Taj. A relief.

Tears slide down my face and Taj uses his thumb to smudge them away. He brushes the back of his hand over my cheek, and then buries his fingers in my hair.

My heart patters as he moves close; his fingertips slip from my cheek to just behind my ear. I close my eyes, waiting. His lips touch mine, feather light, smooth as satin. He pulls away and I open my eyes. Nose to nose, we stare into each other's eyes and a cool breeze licks our faces. Before we can kiss a second time, there is a crash in the bushes behind us, and a group of kids on dirt bikes roar past. We both jump.

"You'll get through this." He leans his head next to mine. "By the way, are you aware of the activities student council has planned for the Spring Fling tonight?"

Oh jeez, I completely forgot the Spring Fling is tonight. "Dancing?"

"Well sure, but besides a DJ, I hear they hired a psychic."

"A psychic?"

CHAPTER EIGHTEEN

Three days, twenty-two hours until the deadline.

The dance. The fact that a psychic is going to be there is an unexpected bonus. My mind races with questions to ask. But at the moment I have a regular girl problem. I'm going to my first dance *with a boy* and I don't have a single thing to wear.

I rummage through my closet. Discarded clothes sail through the air. A blur of browns, blues, and greens land in a huge pile on my bed. My wardrobe is nothing more than tees, jeans, and a few sweaters. And one dress. The dress I wore to Dad's funeral. I rub the black cotton fabric between my fingers. The pockets still bulge with fist-sized wads of tissues. Truth is, I hate this dress. Hate the dress for the purpose it served. I want to get rid of it. Just not quite yet.

Patty waltzes in from the bathroom smelling of strawberry shampoo. A twisted towel twirls around her head like a vanilla custard cone. Her makeup is expertly applied. "Whatcha doin'?"

"Looking for something to wear to the dance tonight." I tuck the black dress back before Patty sees it.

She beams. "You are? Great! Oh Mags, it'll be just like old times. Everyone will be so happy to have you back. Aiden *said* Ethan might ask you. What did he say? Give me all the deets."

I don't answer.

Her expression sours. "Please don't say you're going with that weird boy."

"His name is Taj Mabibbi. And yes, he asked me."

Patty sinks down on her bed. "Are you crazy?"

"Maybe," I answer honestly.

She unwinds the towel from her head and brushes out her damp hair. "Listen Maggie, I know I've been kinda harsh with you lately but it's just because I'm so worried about you. Forget about that guy." She puts down her brush and clasps her hands together like she is just about to offer a little kid some candy. "How 'bout I ask Aiden about Ethan again? If he didn't already ask someone, maybe he can take you tonight. It'll be perfect. Just like we always wanted. I'll call Aiden right now if you promise not to mention any of the weird stuff you've been obsessed with lately. I'll even lend you a dress."

"Us being with the Wilson brothers is what *you* always wanted, Patty. Not me." I push aside the mound of clothes on my bed and sit. "I really like Taj. I don't want to go with anyone else." I fiddle with the hem of a sweater. "Dad would have understood."

"Dad isn't here, so you can't know that. But of course there is no way he would have agreed with me, right?" Patty holds up various dresses, scrutinizing.

"I never said that," I mutter.

"You don't have to. I know you think you and Dad were special, but Dad and I shared lots of things that had nothing to do with you."

"Yeah? Like what?"

"Who do you think took me to the mall and taught me which colors complimented my complexion? Who do you think taught me how to make our grandmother's Irish stew? He even gave me the lowdown on how to tell when a boy likes a girl."

"He did?"

She hangs a dress on the doorknob and pulls the tie on her robe tight. "Dad and I shared special times together too, and I miss him like crazy."

"You don't act like you do."

"Why? 'Cause I'm not walking around boo-hooing all the time? Dad would have wanted us to be strong, to move on."

"But it's so hard."

"Life isn't easy, Maggie. You learn to cope and make the best of things. At least that's what I'm trying to do." Patty slips into a blue T-shirt dress. Her beads jangle like wind chimes as she moves to sit by my side. She sighs. "Go ahead, borrow something. Just remember, I'm only trying to help you."

"I really like Taj, Patty."

"Okay, okay. I hear you. Now get ready."

Patty goes downstairs and I finish dressing. Patty's clothes are pretty, but I need something more. I take the beetle Taj transformed for me and slide a chain through a hook on the end. I slip the necklace over my head and peek at the mirror. Perfect.

Kids swarm the parking lot, girls teeter on rarely worn heels, and guys tug at the collars of their dress shirts. I spy Taj by the gym doors, wearing his black bowler and a gray, pinstriped, three-piece suit. Patty finds Aiden by the tennis courts, and we head in.

Inside, the gymnasium has been transformed into a garden of pink, yellow, and green crepe paper and glitter. A sparkling disco ball hangs in the center of the room, throwing tiny triangles of light across the walls and floor. Sugar and some other girls rush over, giggling, until their eyes land on Taj. They freeze, and their laughter falls away.

"What happened to Ethan?" Sugar asks.

"Not now," Patty answers in a curt tone.

Sugar opens her mouth as if she's about to say something, but then closes it. She grabs the arm of her date; in her three-inch heels Sugar towers over the poor guy. She drags him out to the dance floor.

I gently tug on Taj's arm. "Forget about her. I'm glad I'm here with you."

"Thanks." He pushes a strand of hair out of my eyes. "My beautiful, mysterious Mona Lisa." Then he touches a finger to the glittering beetle. "You wore it."

"Of course, I love it." His dark curls frame his face perfectly, and his soft brown eyes look only at me. I take a deep breath. "You look really good too, Taj."

His cheeks flush. "You don't have to say that, but thanks."

He looks down at me, and I am lost, swimming in his sweet-tea eyes. My pulse races. What if Taj asks me to dance? Of course he will, that's why it's called a dance. I should have gotten some lessons from Patty.

He takes both my hands and squeezes. "I know you really want to see the psychic. I don't blame you. But, I just wanted to say I'm so happy to be here with you." He pulls me closer and moves his hands to either side of my waist. I feel them trembling a bit.

"I'm happy to be here with you, too."

The slow notes of an acoustic guitar accompanied by a piano fill the room. "May I have this dance, m'lady?"

The DJ plays a sweet ballad and I reach up, letting my hands rest on Taj's shoulders. How close do I stand? Which way do I move my feet?

Taj rocks back and forth, slowly stepping in a small circle. I follow and forget about worrying how close to stand or where to put my feet. The chorus, "It was enchanting to meet you," floats through the air, and by then I am floating, too. These words could be mine. Enchanted to find Taj again. My childhood friend, and now so much more.

I sway to the music, encircled by Taj's arms, moving closer and closer, letting the melody wash over me. My head rests on his shoulder; I breathe in cinnamon and soap, and I am in my own little world. Safe.

The music tempo rises and we circle faster, my skirt swishing against my legs as we twirl under the sparkling lights. The room spins; dresses whirl in waves of color, ebbing and flowing. Dizzying. I struggle to stand, but it's as if my feet are being sucked into the sand as the ocean's tide pulls out. A flutter tickles my collarbone, and then the lights dim. My birthmark sizzles.

The lights flicker then turn bright. I look around at the crowd. All I see are women, and none of them are my classmates.

Men enter the room. One of them runs his fingertips over the pistol at his hip; metal skull-shaped badges decorate his hat and collar. "Off with your clothes," his deep voice orders.

Fear clutches me with sharp bony fingers. We look at each other in disbelief. How can he expect us to undress in public? In front of men? I watch as the SS soldier shoves the woman closest to him. She falls to her knees but doesn't make a move to undress. He kicks her in the gut. She rolls to the side, clutching her belly. He approaches her again and she scrambles to untie her shoelaces.

"Clothes to the left. Shoes to the right." He smirks as if proud to have intimidated the poor, defenseless woman.

He turns his icy stare to me, and my stomach drops. I kick off my shoes and toss them to the right side of the room. Looking around, I see everyone reluctantly undressing. I reach down to the hem of my top and begin to lift it . . .

"No, Maggie." Taj grasps my hands and pulls them away; my silk blouse falls back around my waist. Patty grabs my arm and drags me toward the hallway.

My eyes shift left, then right. "What's happening?" I shout, trying to be heard over the blaring music.

The gymnasium door "fwumps" shut behind us, muffling the sound of loud music. Patty drops my arm and hands me my shoes.

"We were dancing and all of a sudden you stopped and stood back. You got that funny look on your face. Like when we had the séance," Taj says.

"Mags, you were doing a striptease in front of the entire class!" Patty grabs my hands. "Thank goodness Taj stopped you."

Kathy Lundy from my art class bursts out of the gym and shoves past us, mascara smeared down her face. She is quickly followed by Michael, her Taurus seatmate, who is waving his hands in the air, apologizing profusely. He turns, looks at me, and smirks. Kathy catches the pause and gives me an evil look, mouthing *slut*.

My God, how far did I go? "Patty?"

"Don't worry, Mags. So you flashed a bit of navel, maybe a little more. No worse than someone in a bikini. But it was really weird. Your face. I can't describe it."

Aiden finds us. His eyebrows are pinched with concern. "Patty?"

"Oh, hey Aiden." She shakes out her hair so it falls in shining waves down her back. "Spider went down my sister's top. Can you believe it? Totally freaked her out."

I nod, impressed with Patty's quick thinking.

"Arachnophobia," Taj says. "Fear of spiders."

"Did you get it?" Aiden asks.

Taj lifts up his boot. "Obliterated under my heel. Didn't stand a chance."

"Good." He rubs his hands together. "Wanna dance some more, Patty?"

Patty turns to me. "Um . . ."

I nod. "I'll be fine. You go."

Patty lets Aiden whisk her away.

I take a deep breath. "The psychic. We need to find her now."

We step over the tangled legs of boys and girls sitting against the wall, waiting in line for the photo booth. We avoid the dark corners where couples make out. When the chaperone walks by, they break apart and shuffle away, only to return moments later.

Where is the psychic? I hope she didn't bail. Then I see a paper sign taped to the door of the classroom at the end of the hall. It reads, "Madame Chandra."

"She's in there!" I point and practically drag Taj over to the classroom.

But when I enter, my smile drops. A silk scarf tied around her head, gypsy-style, Ms. Cherry sits at a black velvet-draped table.

She waves. Her bright purple fingernails glitter like amethysts, and rings encircle every finger. "If it isn't my favorite Aquarius and Gemini. Taj, please turn the sign on my door to 'In Session.'"

"You're the psychic?" I ask, my voice devoid of enthusiasm. I can't believe it. *Just my luck.*

"Do I sense doubt, my independent thinker?" She raises a black eyebrow at me. "Sit down. Believe it or not I am blessed with the gift of second sight. It is both a blessing and a curse, passed on generation after generation to the women of my family." The longer she speaks, the dreamier her voice becomes.

I slump in a chair across from her, using everything in my power not to roll my eyes or burst into tears.

"It is a time of great discovery for you. Perhaps even a bit of romance?" She winks at Taj.

I moan and Taj squeezes my hand.

"I see you working hard. Your painting, perhaps?" She closes her eyes, as if psychic messages are being broadcast against the insides of her eyelids. "I see duplicity in you. It's confusing now, but the answer you seek will soon make itself clear."

I tap my foot. "Is that all?"

"Good things are in store for you, dear soul. You must be patient."

I turn to Taj and finally roll my eyes.

Ms. Cherry opens her eyelids and leans forward. "Do you have any questions?" She twists one of her gaudy rings around her finger.

What the heck, I'll take a chance. "Do you see anyone around me?" As in the ghost who's been haunting the heck out of me?

Ms. Cherry puts a finger to her temple and closes her eyes, again consulting the teleprompter in her head. I notice one of her fake eyelashes coming unattached. Her forehead crinkles. The corners of her lips turn down. "Pain. Such intense pain." She snaps open her eyes. Her mouth twists into a grimace. "I'm not joking. This is real." She shoves up the sleeve of her cotton blouse and rubs her left arm. "Right here." But nothing is there. It isn't even red.

Taj shifts in his chair. "Ms. Cherry, do you have any problems with your heart? Pain in the left arm can sometimes indicate—"

"Owww," I shriek. My left forearm burns, stinging over and over like a knife stabbing me. Sticking, twisting, red-hot pain. I yank up my sleeve. "My arm!"

Taj and Ms. Cherry lean in close.

First the letter "A," then numerals, 1 . . . 8 . . . 3 . . . 3 . . . 7 flow across my left forearm, light green at first, then darkening to a deep teal.

Ms. Cherry's arms drop to her sides. Her jaw hangs open. "Maggie, what's happening?"

Taj isn't staring at my arm anymore. He is looking into my eyes. We both know what they did to prisoners in Auschwitz. It is true. The coat girl is really here.

Taj grabs my right hand and pulls me to my feet. "Invisible ink. Bought it at a magic shop. Supposed to materialize like magic." He laughs awkwardly. "Worked. But it appears Maggie may be allergic to it. Better get her home."

"See, I sensed the allergic reaction in my own arm. I'm a bit of an empath, too. Feel better, Maggie," Ms. Cherry calls after us.

We rush down the hallway, our footsteps echoing against the lockers. We keep running until we reach the parking lot. Under the yellow glow of the lights I examine my arm more closely. The burn is not as intense now, but it still aches, throbbing right down to the bone.

"Does it hurt?" Taj asks. His fingers hover just above the spot.

I swipe my hand across the green letter and numbers, but they don't smear or change. The deep heat rises to a boil when I touch it. "Oww, yeah. Hurts."

I pull my hand back, lean my head against Taj's warm shoulder, and close my eyes. Please, when I open them again, let everything be back to normal and I'll realize this was all a horrible dream.

But when I open my eyes, the tattoo is still there.

A 1 8 3 3 7.

CHAPTER NINETEEN
Three days, nine hours until the deadline.

Taj walks me home. We reach my front porch and the living room curtains shift. Mom.

"Are you going to be okay? I mean your arm. I could—"

"It feels a little better."

Silence. Taj shuffles his feet. "So?"

I stand on my toes and he bends his head toward me. Our lips meet. My hand reaches up for his curls. His arms are around my waist.

The porch light flicks on and Taj backs up a step. Both of us blink in the sudden brightness.

"I guess I better get going."

I nod. "See you tomorrow."

"Goodnight, Maggie."

I fall asleep realizing the tattoo, although painful and scary, is the best clue the coat girl has given me. It is also proof that my mind has not been the culprit in the recent weird happenings, which is a relief. Wish her timing was a little better, though.

All I need to do is find the name that corresponds with the number inked on my arm.

I still have three full days left to finish my painting. I haven't broken my promise to my dad yet.

After I get home from church, Taj and I scour the Internet and the library records, hoping to find the identity of prisoner A18337. Matching a name to the tattooed number on my arm is not an easy task. Seems most of the records are in Germany and not searchable through the Internet. The best we can do is to fill out a form and mail it to the address of the agency holding the information. But the website says it will take at least eight weeks to receive a reply. I'd better kiss any hopes of attending the Peabody Academy goodbye. If my dad is watching me, I hope he knows how sorry I feel.

I drop the letter in the mailbox on my way to Silver Lake. I called Mrs. Valentine earlier this morning. Miss Berk is still in the hospital, but I have an idea. Maybe I can still solve the mystery and finish my painting.

Taj has to go home to help his father, so my next adventure will be done solo. He bids me farewell with a sweet, cinnamon kiss.

I need to gather more clues about Gittel and the coat girl. I feel a bit like a creeper planning it, but I don't think I have a choice. I have little more than two days to turn in my painting to the Peabody Arts Council.

The crux of my plan is safely folded inside my backpack: a get-well card I made for Miss Berk. I creak open the front door of the home. It's so quiet. Miss Berk's absence makes me feel empty. Alone. I didn't realize how attached I am to the old woman.

"Maggie," Mrs. Valentine calls from down the hall. She hurries over, her cherubic face breaking into a smile. "How are you, dear?"

"Fine. How's Miss Berk?"

She nervously smooths her hair with her pudgy hand. "Gittel is hard as nails. She'll bounce back in no time."

"I made her a card." I sling my backpack over one shoulder and reach around, unzipping it to pull out the card.

"Beautiful, honey. You are such a sweet girl." She pats me on the head like a puppy.

"Would it be okay if I bring it up to her room? I'll put it on her night table so she'll be sure to see it the minute she comes home." I know Mrs. Valentine has strict rules about the residents' privacy, but maybe . . .

"You know my policy, dear." She pats me again and holds out her hand. "I'll take it up to her room after I finish with the breakfast dishes." Mrs. Valentine disappears into the kitchen and I stand in the hallway, unsure what to do.

"Psst." Suzi peeks her head around the parlor doorway. "Does this room visit have anything to do with the spooky tale you told me about that old tweed coat?"

I nod. Suzi disappears for a moment, then returns with a ring of keys. She shrugs. "Must have sticky fingers." She waves me toward the staircase. "Come on, let's go sleuthing, Scooby."

We find Miss Berk's room, turn the key in the lock, and slip inside. Her room is spare, a light oak dresser against one wall, a bed covered with a blue quilted blanket across from the dresser, and a glider rocker in front of a small television. Not much in the way of clues.

Suzi plops down on the bed. "So do I have to ask? I'm dying here."

"What?"

"Your boy. Did tall, dark, and handsome kiss you yet?"

I smile and lower my eyes. "Yeh, he did."

She falls back on the bed and kicks her feet in the air, then pops back up. "Ohhhhhh, was it wonderfully, magically, swoon-worthy? Any tongue?"

"Suzi!" I smack her arm, then join her on the bed and lay back. "It was pretty magical."

She falls back and fans herself. "Oooohhh, be still my heart."

"Okay, enough of this." I sit up and open my backpack. "We have work to do. Your grandmother said she'd bring the card up after she finished the dishes."

"Oh, okay. But I want a detailed report later."

I open Miss Berk's dresser drawers and search, but find only sweaters and underwear. Suzi roots around in the closet.

"Anything?" I ask.

"Nada." She frowns. "It's almost too clean. Like she is deliberately hiding her past. What if she was an international spy?"

"Guess we won't find out until she gets better." Should I tell her about the Auschwitz connection or keep it to myself?

"Wait, let me check under the bed."

Suzi drops to the floor and wriggles under the bed frame, and sneezes.

"God bless you."

"Thanks. Nothing but dust bunnies running around under here. She squirms in a little farther. "Wait. I think I see something." She wiggles a little more. "Got it. Now pull me out before I suffocate to death."

I grab her ankles and pull. Her hair is a buzzing hive of static laced with dust motes.

"Lookie here."

She hands me a book. With the edge of my sleeve, I dust it off. The word "Diary" is embossed in gold script letters across the cover. I sit on the edge of Miss Berk's bed, the leather-bound book on my lap. The angel on my right shoulder says, "Reading someone's diary is way wrong, Maggie McConnell," but the devil on the left screams, "Jackpot!" I touch the diary's little gold latch and long to pop it open, but I don't.

"Now this is what I'm talkin' about." Suzi grins.

She reaches for the book, but I pull it back. "It's her diary. Her private thoughts."

"And the best darn clue we could have found." Suzi grabs the diary and opens it. I lunge for it, but she dances away. "Phooey, it's written in some crazy language, and I don't think my two years of Latin will help me decipher it." She hands the book to me. "Take it home and find someone who can read it."

I run my fingers across the soft leather. *I want this book.* I clutch the diary to my chest. Maybe I'll take it home and have a tiny peek. I know I can find a translator program on my computer. It might hold a clue, after all, and isn't that why I was sneaking around Miss Berk's room in the first place? *But this is wrong, wrong, wrong!* Just as I am about to shove the book back under the bed, we hear a bang in the hall. I cram the diary into my backpack and Suzi and I dive under the bed.

Stale air and dust surround us like a fog of gnats.

"What about the keys," I whisper. "Won't she notice them missing?"

"Took the spares. What, do you think I'm an amateur or something?"

The doorknob squeaks, and then the door creaks open. "Hmm, this is strange. I'm sure I locked the door. Hope *I'm* not going senile," Mrs. Valentine says to herself.

Suzi stifles a giggle. I nudge her in the side. Mrs. Valentine's brown loafers shuffle toward us, moving closer to the nightstand. "There, the card looks perfect. Such a sweet girl. Gittel will love it."

My guilty conscience causes perspiration to drip down my back like I just ran a marathon. The sores across my back burn from the salty sweat and I have to stifle a cry of pain. Mrs. Valentine's feet disappear from view. The door closes with a whoosh, and the lock clicks into place.

We pull our dusty selves out from under the bed. "I'll go downstairs and distract Grams. When I start singing, you skidaddle."

I wait at the top of the steps, listening.

"Scooby, dooby, doo, where are you?" Suzi croons the cartoon's theme song. *Good one, Suzi.* I slink down the steps like the rat I am.

What came over me? Stealing a sweet old lady's diary? I should be talking to her in person, not snooping around for personal secrets. Even though my backpack is relatively light, it is as if I'm shouldering a ton of bricks. But even though I know it is wrong, I'm going to read it as soon as I get home.

CHAPTER TWENTY
Two days, eighteen hours until the deadline.

Upstairs in my room, I withdraw the soft leather diary from my backpack and open it. Little scraps of papers are pasted to the pages. On the first page, I read.

20 navember 1942

In nakht ikh khlum fun meyn mshpkhh, demolt ikh vekn tsu dem lebedik genem. Vi ken dos pasirn? Ikh viln meyn alt lebn tsurik desperatli. Tomer meyn vaking lebn iz nor a shlekht khlum.

Is this written in German? I jump on the computer and type the entire text in, then run it through a translator program. It comes up Yiddish.

It says:

November 20, 1942

At night I dream of my family, then I wake to this living hell. How could this happen? I want my old life back desperately. Perhaps my waking life is just a bad dream.

November 27, 1942

I look at the guards. The men in dark coats with skulls on their caps. Their eyes are cold like balls of ice. Were they always so? Some seem to fleetingly melt and I'll see a trace of humanity. Then the moment passes and they become like their comrades.

December 5, 1942

They shaved our heads, but bugs still crawl over our skin and bite us in our sleep.

Rats and mice are constant bedtime companions. If only Minka were here to keep guard over me.

Minka. Gittel's cat.

December 10, 1942

Today I am assigned to work as a laundress. I am so pleased that my best friend Freyda was sent along with me.

Freyda? Freyda is the name Miss Berk always calls me when she's out of it.

It means no more hours of roll call out in the freezing cold. Only thirty or so girls work in the laundry facility and the Kapo takes roll call inside.

She seems nicer than the last guard, but I still don't trust her. Kapos are Jews but even your own can turn on you in this horrid place.

They feed us better here. We need our strength to do our job. We wash the clothes of the officers and their families.

My hands are so dry and sore from the blisters that never seem to heal.

We have to dunk the clothes in steaming hot water and then hang them up outside.

The temperature in the yard is freezing and the change from hot to cold makes my hands burn with pain.

Yes. I saw this in the dryer vision.

Ech, my lips are chapped and bleeding from the freezing cold, but I know I have it much better than others.

January 2, 1943

There was an announcement today. Frau Hoess needs two girls to design and sew dresses for her. They will live in the Hoess's attic.

I am not sure if that is a good or bad thing. To sleep under the same roof as the Monster.

Freyda and I are considered the most talented and were taken away by Frau Hoess. Thank God, I get to stay with my friend.

I hope everyone keeps us in their prayers.

After that entry, the pages are blank.

Ohmigod, Freyda! Is Freyda the coat girl?

I dash into the studio. "Freyda! Are you Freyda?" I shout at the portrait. Nothing. I try painting again, but Freyda's ghost still sends debilitating quakes through my hands. Now I know the coat girl's name, but it is still not enough. She needs something more. And I don't know what.

I have a million questions to ask Miss Berk. Is the girl Freyda from the diary the same Freyda Miss Berk is always remembering? What happened to her? Why is she haunting me? But I know I am getting closer, and I still have two days and eighteen hours left to complete my painting. I have to make the deadline.

Last night I filled Taj in on the secrets I uncovered in Miss Berk's diary, and we made plans to meet today in the park, and then visit Silver Lake. I need to return the diary. I am still a little ashamed of violating the code of privacy. I bring along the tweed coat, just in case.

My fuzzy blue sweater covers the tattoo on my arm as I race to the park to meet Taj. He paces under the shade of a huge oak. Perched on his head is the same blue newsboy cap he wore on the first day I saw him. I remember how weird I thought it looked. Now I can't get over how cute it is. I sneak up behind him and cover his eyes, trying to suppress my giggles. His eyelashes flutter against my palms. "Guess who?"

"I don't know." He laughs. "Could be any of the trillion girls who planned to meet me in the park."

"A trillion, huh." I let go and he faces me. "Sorry, just me, plain old boring Maggie."

He takes my hand and presses it to his lips with a kiss. "Believe me, m'lady. You are far from boring."

I think he means that in a good way. Actually, I am sure of it.

At Silver Lake we meet Mrs. Valentine in the foyer and I introduce her to Taj. She shakes his hand and winks at me. "Suzi will be sorry she missed you." I wonder how much Suzi has told her grandmother about my love life.

"Maggie, I was going to call you, dear. I know how worried you were about Miss Berk."

"Is she home from the hospital?" I hold my breath, conscious of the weight of the tweed coat in the bag hanging on my arm.

"She arrived this morning. She was asking for you, dear."

I squeeze Taj's hand. "She was?"

"Why don't you go upstairs and say hello. But keep your visit brief, hon. She still needs her rest."

Hand in hand, Taj and I start up the creaky steps. Questions swirl around in my head, mixing and blending so thoroughly I'm not sure what to ask first.

CHAPTER TWENTY-ONE

One day, twenty-three hours until the deadline.

I barely recognize Miss Berk. Her hair flows like snowdrifts over her shoulders and around her milky white face.

"Hi, Miss Berk. Mrs. Valentine says you're feeling better. I hope I'm not bothering you." Taj stands slightly behind me. I tug on his sleeve and pull him to my side. He takes the blue newsboy cap off his head, revealing a serious case of hat-head. I reach up and fluff his hair a bit. "This is my friend, Taj."

Miss Berk's eyes, dull and blank a moment ago, sparkle. "Hello, dear. Nice to meet you, young man."

Taj bows. "The pleasure is all mine."

"How do you feel?" I ask.

Her voice is faint. She pulls a pink crocheted shawl around her shoulders. "I'm much better, thank you. And thank you for the beautiful card."

"You're welcome. I tried to draw a picture of what your kitten Minka might have looked like."

A look of sadness crosses her face. "Ah, Minka, she was such a beautiful cat. I hated to leave her." She pulls her shawl tighter as if protecting herself from a bad memory. "Your card was perfect." She smiles. "I'm glad you're here. I wanted to tell you how sorry I am about the way I acted the other day when I saw your painting." She looks from Taj to me. "It reminded me of—" Her hands fiddle with the fringe on her shawl. "Something from my past." Her gaze falls. "You couldn't have known."

"I might have some idea," I reply. "Can you tell me more about Freyda?"

She looks surprised. "Freyda? My best friend Freyda Grossman?"

"Yes." I choose my words carefully so I don't upset her. "Did your friend Freyda own a tweed coat with a fur collar?" I pull the coat from the bag and lay it next to her.

Miss Berk's eyes open wide and her mouth forms a little "o." She reaches toward the coat and runs her wrinkled hands over the fabric. "Freyda loved this coat so much. It was a birthday gift from her father. He smuggled it in, you know. Her birthday fell during Hanukkah that year. She was so excited. But, how did you find it? It was up in the attic and—"

Hanukkah. That explains the eight lit candles I saw in the mirror the first time I tried on the coat. The clue makes perfect sense now.

"Mrs. Valentine was doing some rearranging up there."

She brings the coat close to her nose. "Mmm, still smells of Chanel Number Five." She laughs; her low cackle becomes breathier until it is a full-fledged wheeze. She has to stop and find her voice. "Oh, such a fit Freyda's mother had when Freyda found where her mother had hidden her prized perfume and tried to sneak a dab and ended up practically spilling half the bottle on this coat." She sniffs the coat again. "Still smells good." She looks up at me with moist gray eyes. "But how did you know?"

I take hold of her hand. Her skin is tissue-thin and soft. "I think Freyda's ghost may be haunting this coat."

Miss Berk's eyes crinkle, and a smile spreads across her face as she gives my hand a squeeze. "Honey, there are no such thing as ghosts."

Good, she seems to be taking the news well. "I know it's hard to believe. I didn't believe it myself in the beginning, but ever since I found this coat, strange things have been happening to me." I lower my voice. "I think Freyda's ghost has been coming to me in my dreams. And it's not just dreams. I've been seeing things through her eyes while I'm wide awake."

"Hallucinations," Taj adds.

"Your young man is very handsome," Miss Berk whispers to me with a wink.

I look away, my face flushing.

When I turn back to Miss Berk, her eyes go cloudy. Darn, I've lost her to the past again. "You always did attract the most handsome young men, Freyda."

Um, not really true for *me*, but I don't argue. I want to know more about this Freyda, but are Miss Berk's memories reliable in this mental state?

I sit on the edge of her bed and take her hands in mine. "Miss Berk, Miss Berk, I really need to know more about Freyda." The mist clears; her eyes turn bright, as if a light has been flicked on.

"Yes, my dear friend Freyda. Poor Freyda and I went through the most horrific time of our lives together." Her eyes look distant, remembering. I'm afraid I might lose her any minute.

"What happened to Freyda?" Taj asks.

Miss Berk's gaze falls on the window. Tears gather. "We worked for the Monster's wife, Frau Hoess. At Auschwitz."

Taj and I exchange looks.

"She kept us like dogs up in the attic. A blanket tossed on the hard wood floor was our bed. Moldy bread and thin soup for our suppers. The days and nights seemed to run on forever. We couldn't spend the rest of our lives that way. It was slowly killing us. One day we peeked out the small attic window and noticed the dogs that normally guarded the grounds were being loaded into a truck. They were taking them out of the compound—"

My birthmark stabs me like a hot poker. The searing heat blasts through my chest. I clutch at it, fall into Taj's arms, and the room turns black.

I am in the dusty attic. With all my might I force open the small window.

"Come on, Gittel. We can make it. The tree branch is hanging close enough to the roof now. We might not get another chance."

"But the dogs. They'll shred us to pieces."

"No. I heard the men outside the window earlier today. The dogs are getting veterinary checkups tonight. But we must hurry. They could be back any time."

"But what if they come back before we get far enough away? We'll die."

"If we die, we die. It's our only chance. We have to take it."

I scramble out onto the roof, hooking my fingers around the slate shingles and moving crab-like toward a large fir tree. I look over at the window and see Gittel's dirty brown boot emerging over the sill. I move my foot to the next hold, but it slips. The slate dislodges, falling to the ground with a loud CRACK.

Heart pounding, I freeze and hug my body close to the roof, trying to become a part of the structure. When I'm sure we haven't attracted attention, I grab hold of the hanging tree branch and pull myself up.

I see Gittel clinging to the side of the roof, trembling. "Gittel, just take it slow. You can do it."

"I'm scared," she squeaks.

I hold out my hand, and she inches closer. Our fingers are almost touching when she loses her footing and slips down the roof. She is about to go over the edge when her fingers grasp the gutter ledge. Dirt and leaves scatter to the ground.

"Freyda!" she shouts.

Below us, the door opens and light spills onto the front lawn. I hold my breath.

"Who's out there?" Frau Hoess shouts.

The whip marks on my back pulse with the sound of her voice. The tree bark bites into my hands, but I dare not move. I glance over at Gittel clinging to the copper gutter. Her eyes scream panic.

But the door closes. Gittel scrambles toward me and catches my hand, and I haul her onto the branch. We shimmy down the tree and duck under a bush. Wasting no time, we tear across the compound and search for the road. The electric barbed wire fence behind the house buzzes, as if it were crying. We need to distance ourselves from that sound.

When we reach a large field, I smell water. The river must be near. We can follow it to freedom. Our bodies are weak and not used to so much activity. Gittel holds her side, panting.

"There's no time to rest, Gittel. We must keep moving."

She nods and jogs toward me, still holding her side. I feel bad for her. Perhaps we could take a short break. It feels as if we've been running for hours.

Then we hear a shout, followed by a deep bark. The dogs! We are exposed, with nowhere to hide.

A man with a flashlight finds our faces. "Stupid Jews." In the circle of light I can see there is just one dog. But one dog is plenty to get the job done.

"Please, please leave us be," Gittel begs.

The guard grabs us by our necks and gives us a push. "Back to the barracks." He doesn't realize we belong to Frau Hoess.

"I'm going to distract him," I whisper to Gittel. "When I do, run to the river. The dog will lose your scent in the water. Go back to the caves. I'll find you—I promise."

Gittel shakes her head, but I know we are only in this situation because of my recklessness. If anyone is to be punished, it should be me.

I twist my body around and clamp my teeth on the guard's wrist. He yelps and lets go of Gittel. The dog locks onto my leg, shaking it back and forth. I bite my tongue to keep from crying out. I don't want Gittel returning to help me. From the corner of my eye I see her disappear into the shadows.

When I open my eyes again, I am sitting by Miss Berk's bed, Taj's arms around me.

"She's showing me things," I say. "As if they were my memories. But why?"

"Yes, you were recounting the story out loud, Maggie," says Taj.

"They are your memories, Freyda." Tears stream down Miss Berk's face. "You did it. You really did it. You came back to me, just like you said you would. You do remember your promise, yes?"

"Promise?" I take a deep breath. "What promise? I remember promising to make a gown. A white gown. It was chiffon, like the one in my painting." When I speak, my voice sounds like it comes from someone else far away.

"Chiffon? Yes." Gittel's gray eyes darken. "Of course I remember the dress. They demanded we complete two garments before twelve sharp each Saturday. I had fallen behind, and—"

"You changed places with me. You took three lashings for being late with the dress."

"You were sick with fever. So weak—" I stop. My voice catches.

Gittel pushes herself up with her frail arms and her shawl slips from her shoulders. "You did keep your promise. You'll remember."

I'm still confused. "Look at this." I push up my sleeve and hold out my arm. Gittel traces the numbers with one finger, then pulls up her own sleeve and shows me her tattoo. Hers is one number off. "You came right after me. You are Freyda."

I look closely at Gittel's eyes. No mistiness clouds them.

My scalp prickles. My eyes rest on the coat draped over Gittel's knees. "But the tweed coat. How—" I start.

"I followed the river. Found the caves again. The coat was right where you'd hidden it. You loved it so much, I couldn't leave it there. When I escaped to the United States I took it with me. I've held onto it all these years, believing . . . but where—"

"Mrs. Valentine was cleaning out the things in storage in her attic. She gave all the stuff, including the coat, to the Salvation Army Thrift Shop. That's where I found it. It called to me." I gather the coat in my arms and bury my nose in the tweed fabric. Memories of a kind, dark-haired woman flash in my mind. "*Mama, I miss you.*" The words come out of my mouth as if they are my own. My entire body shakes.

Miss Berk hugs me close and her arms around me are as familiar as the tweed coat. Her hot tears flow against my cheek. "Freyda, my dear friend."

I go limp as a rag doll as Gittel rocks me in her arms.

Have I become Freyda? Or has Freyda become me?

There is a soft rap on the door. "Maggie, Miss Berk needs her rest. You can visit again tomorrow, dear," Mrs. Valentine calls.

I don't want to leave. I need to know more.

Taj puts his hand on my shoulder. I forgot he was even there. "She's looking really pale. I think maybe she should rest."

Reluctantly, I stand. I don't want to let go of Gittel's hands. Inch by inch our fingers slide apart. "Rest, I'll be back. We have so much more to talk about."

"I love you, my dear friend," Gittel says as I close the door.

Taj leads me out of Silver Lake. "Come on, Maggie."

Maggie.

My mind unravels. Thoughts fly loose, then tangle again. Who is Maggie? Has Maggie been replaced?

CHAPTER TWENTY-TWO

One day, twenty hours until the deadline.

It's raining as we walk back from Silver Lake. Memories of my life as Freyda freeze like ice and then turn slushy, ebbing and flowing in the river of time: My hair being shaved, drifting to the floor in soft clumps. Hunger, a hot coal burning in my belly. Cold chilling me inside and out. Whippings splitting my skin.

I see a little girl with kohl eyes and dark hair. The men with the black boots and long coats took her. My sister, Rebecca?

When the ice of the past re-forms, the heat of Taj's voice brings me back to the present.

"We're at your house, Maggie," Taj says. Raindrops collect in my bangs and drip into my eyes. He smooths back my hair from my forehead. His arm is warm around my waist, and my toes squish inside my sneakers as he leads me up the porch steps. I stumble twice but he holds me tight. My eyes are no longer clouded by rain but continue to view the world through a fogged pane.

Patty opens the front door and rushes forward as we reach the top steps. "Maggie, what happened?"

Without saying a word, I slip past her and collapse on the sofa.

"What's wrong with her?" She drapes Mom's soft afghan over me and I pull it around my shoulders. Taj sits next to me, folding my trembling hand in his. "I think she's in shock."

"Shock? What did you do to her?" Patty rushes to my other side, feeling my forehead and searching my eyes.

"Nothing. I'd never hurt her." He draws me closer and rubs my back in small circles, warming me, keeping me with him.

Patty kneels in front of me and looks into my eyes, searching for an explanation.

I meet her gaze and my mouth moves. "I had another sister," I murmur, my voice small and faraway. "Her name was Becca . . ."

A flash of fear crosses Patty's face as she turns to Taj. "What's she talking about?"

Taj stops rubbing my back and squeezes my hand. "You should tell her."

"Tell me what?" Patty leans closer.

I close my eyes for a moment and force myself to concentrate. "We found the owner of the tweed coat."

Patty straightens up and tosses back her hair. "Oh, I should have known it had something to do with that awful thing. I hope you gave it back."

My focus falters, swimming in and out. *I see the man I call Father, but not from this lifetime; I know this is Freyda's father. He has the same dark eyes and hair, the same curve to his mouth as she does.*

He holds out a big box. I take it, tossing aside the cardboard top and unfolding the crinkly white tissue paper. My fingers dig into the soft fur collar.

Behind him, a menorah flickers. "Happy birthday, my darling girl."

Taj shakes my shoulders gently and I return to the present. Patty holds a glass to my mouth and I take a sip.

"Freyda's sister was Rebecca. She died." My voice cracks on the last word.

"What's wrong with her, Taj?" Patty demands.

I lean forward. "I'm becoming her. The ghost. I'm becoming Freyda."

Patty folds her arms. "Mags, you are you." She turns to Taj. "What's she talking about?"

"The ghost haunting the coat is named Freyda," he begins, "and . . ."

"Enough. This is ridiculous." Patty says. "I think you need to go."

"But . . ."

"Now." Patty says in a low tone.

Taj raises his hands in surrender and walks backward toward the door. "I'll give you two your privacy, but I'm just a call away, Maggie. Call me if you need me, no matter what time of the day or night." Patty jumps up and rushes him out the door.

She returns and guides me toward the stairs. "You need to forget all this nonsense, Maggie. You need rest. Things will look clearer in the morning."

When I wake, Patty is asleep on her side of the room. I slip deeper under my covers. My left arm itches, and as I scratch, the itch turns to a slow burn. I draw it out from under the blankets.

"Patty!" I cry.

Patty springs from her bed and clicks on the light on my night table.

"Look!" I hold out my arm.

We watch, bug-eyed, as the numbers on my arm fade from dark green to light green to nothing at all. I rub the place where the numbers had been. The burning pain is gone, too.

Patty touches the spot. "Whatever that was it must have worn off."

"But you saw it. It just disappeared."

"Disappeared. Wore off. Who cares? It's gone now, and that's that."

Maybe it's all over now. "Now that Freyda found Gittel, maybe her ghost is gone," I say.

"Maggie, think logically. There are no such things as ghosts. You were under a lot of stress. I know Dad's death hit you really hard. The mind can do crazy things."

"Crazy things like what happened to Aunt Bridget?"

"Nothing like that. Aunt Bridget was very sick. Are you worried you have what she had? I don't think you do, but if it would make you feel better, we can talk to Mom about it in the morning." Patty holds out her arms. "Mags, come here." She puts her arm around me. "I am your sister, Patty. You are Maggie. You're okay now."

Yes, I am Maggie and Patty is my sister, and she loves me. I shouldn't think about anything else.

After a few moments, Patty lets go of me and I climb back into bed. The moon shines in our window, making the same familiar patterns on the floor, but it is as if I am seeing everything through new eyes. "Love you much, Patty."

"Love you more." Patty's voice floats from the other side of the room.

Who am I? Can this be more than a haunting? The question rattles in my head like the radiator beside my bed. The pine tree outside our window blows against the siding. The familiar sounds of my life and my home tug at me.

The night sounds eventually lull me to sleep.

Chapter Twenty-Three

Last full day before the deadline.

The sun is shining and the world looks so normal. Even the air seems lighter, fresher. Last night was crazy. Maybe Patty was right. It was probably all stress. Today I feel like my old self. I need to distance myself from Gittel and all the confusion for a few days and concentrate on finishing my painting.

I strain to lift the window in Dad's studio. The stale air rushes out and the scents of fresh grass and pine float in on a warm breeze. On my palette I squeeze out burnt sienna, raw umber, ultramarine blue, titanium white, and viridian green. I have no worries. Somehow I know I'll be able to paint now.

My lines are sure and unwavering. I rough in the background and sketch a huge, arching gate over my portrait. I know exactly what I want to draw.

I pour all of my confusion, frustration, and questions into my work. The archway I am painting was the entrance to the Auschwitz death camp. I remember it from the books Taj and I looked at in the library, but it flickers like a real thing in my memory. The scents of gunpowder, sweat, and rot surround me. I push them away. I refuse to believe the memory belongs to me.

Scrolled in ironwork across the arch reads the phrase *Arbeit Macht Frei*, or Work Makes You Free—an empty promise the Nazis made to people like Miss Berk. The words make my blood boil. Almost involuntarily, I ghost out the letters and write over top: *Mine Neshome Iz Alts Bkhinem*. I study the strange words and know in my heart what they mean: My Soul is Always Free. The phrase fills me with peace.

My entire body aches for the girl in my painting. Even if she isn't a ghost, even if she isn't anybody, this piece is deeply personal. I color the sky magenta and sprinkle it with cinnamon stars—a representation of my blushing, freckled face.

The next morning, I dry the still-damp spots on my painting with a hairdryer, and carefully lift it from the easel. Taj and I are meeting Ms. Cherry at Taj's studio so she can take our work to the competition. He waits by the cemetery gate. I keep the painting facing in. I'm not sure if I'm ready to share yet. As we walk to his studio, I see him eyeing my painting.

"How are you today?" Taj asks. "Any more memories?"

Any more? I can't seem to stop them. It's as if a dam has burst and the floodwaters have not yet receded. I'm determined to ride it out, though. Eventually the memories, if that is what they are, will dry up and life will go back to normal. "I really don't want to talk about it, Taj. It's not real. It's my overactive imagination. That's all."

"Have you ever thought about reincarnation?"

Reincarnation? I don't know what sounds crazier, that or a ghost. "Come on, Taj. Really?"

"Really, Maggie. I haven't slept a wink since I last saw you. I've been spending every minute reading about reincarnation. Did you know there is a little boy who remembers being a fighter pilot in World War II? At age five he could identify the kind of plane he flew and even the spot where it went down."

"Maybe his parents watched lots of war movies."

"He even knew his full name from his past life. They researched it. The name he gave them was the name of a pilot who died in the exact spot he described. His parents found the sister of the man. She was pretty old, but the little boy walked in and acted as if he'd known her all his life. Even called her by the nickname her dead brother used. It's all on YouTube."

"Okay, Taj. That is freaky, but it's a YouTube video—not the most reliable source."

As we reach the studio, Ms. Cherry rumbles up in her old Ford, cuts the engine, and hops out. "How are my inspired artists doing today?"

My face twitches into a fake smile. "Great," I say, trying to sound cheerful.

She raises one of her dark painted eyebrows.

Taj opens the studio door and I escape inside, followed by Ms. Cherry.

"Well, my busy bees. Let's see what you've created."

Taj pulls a sheet off his sculpture and it gleams in the pale light.

Ms. Cherry examines his work from every angle. "This is stunning. Absolutely stunning. Much more powerful than the drawings you showed me."

Taj toes the floor. "Thanks." He peeks up at me. "Can we see yours now, Maggie?"

Slowly, I turn my painting around and place it on an easel Taj has set up by the window.

I hear them both draw in their breath quickly. "Wow," Taj whispers.

"My God, Maggie McConnell. This painting is simply haunting," Ms. Cherry exclaims. "Please tell me more about it."

"She was a girl who was imprisoned in Auschwitz."

"I see the patch on her coat. Yes, go on."

I stare at the painting. I can't form words. The rose-colored background sets off the swirl of chestnut curls caught in the wind. Glints of light flick through her hair. Her face is flushed, full of life. Her eyes are penetrating. Her eyes know me, and I feel as if I know her. "She's searching . . . she's lost . . . .she . . ." The studio lights fade.

My dark-haired mother twists off her wedding ring and carefully folds it in wax paper. She places the parcel in the pocket formed by the hem of her good wool coat.

"What are you doing, Mother?" I ask.

Her expression is pained. "Being prudent, dear, in case we have no choice." Tears run down her face. "Tomorrow morning we will meet Gittel's family in the woods behind the farms. It's not safe here anymore."

"What will we do in the woods? What will we eat? How will we live?" My voice rises with each question.

"We'll be fine," she says, her voice overly bright and unconvincing. "Now here." Mother pulls out the locket Father had helped me get her for her fortieth birthday. "Take this and hide it in your coat. As long as you have this locket, your family will always be with you."

I open the gold filigreed oval and examine its contents. On one side is the photograph of me. I remember it had been a windy day and my hair looked a bit mussed. On the other side is a photograph of my bubbe with her arm around my mother. I bite my lower lip to hold back tears and close the locket. "But, Mother . . ."

"No discussions, Go!" A sob escapes her lips.

I turn to fetch my sewing kit, but Mother takes hold of my arm, stopping me. "If—" A tear slides from the corner of my mother's eye. "If something happens to me, to us, you must run. Run and don't look back."

"But . . ."

"Promise me! You must promise to stay safe!"

"Yes, I promise, Mama. I will stay safe." I promise. The words circle 'round and 'round in my head.

"Good girl, Freyda," she answers.

I run to my room with the tweed coat and sewing kit. With careful stitches, I secure Mother's locket in the seam of the collar. I hold it out for inspection. No one would ever know it is there.

I climb into bed. Across the room rests a small, dark-haired girl. My sister, Becca.

"Love you much, Freyda."

"Love you more, Becca," I say.

The sun is just beginning to rise. A loud bang makes me jump, and I freeze. The bang is followed by screams and the sound of smashing glass. Rushing to my window, I look out to the street below. Hitler's men run door to door, pulling people out of their homes. I see my little sister Rebecca dash out of the house after Gittel's kitten. One of the Nazis boots the cat, sending it flying. Rebecca turns and kicks the man in the shins. He spins, catching her by her long, dark hair and smashes the butt of his gun into her skull. He drops her limp body on the street. A pool of blood seeps around her, coloring the ground crimson. My stomach heaves and its contents rise, burning my throat.

Becca!

I hurry toward the door, but stop at the sound of shouting and heavy boots. Silently, I slip inside my armoire. I search in the dark for a weapon. My hands find my knitting bag. I grab a long needle and hold it tight with both hands.

Moments later my bedroom door bangs open and hits the wall like a gunshot. Someone smashes the furniture. The door to my hiding spot swings open, and from my hiding place behind the clothes, I see boots. Tall, black boots.

I hug the back wall of the closet, poised to plunge the needle into the horrible man's eyes. Someone shouts in the hall and the man leaves my room.

Tremors shake my body as I cower in the oak armoire for hours. Eventually, I gather the courage to leave my safe spot. They might come back, I think. Peeking out the window, I see the streets are empty. They're gone, but I don't see Becca. Papa must have grabbed her. I hope she wasn't hurt too badly. My hand relaxes on the sill.

I have to get to the woods. My family and Gittel's are probably waiting for me, and I don't want to delay them. I take the tweed coat from my closet, rip off the yellow star they'd made me sew on to the left lapel, and slip my arms into the satin sleeves. I tiptoe over the shattered glass and splintered wood.

Downstairs, I find my mother in the kitchen, pale and lifeless. An odd mewling sound escapes my throat as I stare, immobile. Mama's dress is ripped and stained with blood. I drop down beside her and lay my head on her chest. She is so cold. Mama hated the cold.

"Don't worry, Mama. I'll keep you warm." I find a blanket and wrap it around her, gently, the way she'd always tucked me in at night. She would never tuck me in again. My shoulders shake with sobs.

My father is in his study. I know it is Father from the clothes he is wearing, but he has been beaten so badly, he barely resembles himself. I want to remember him smiling and proud, so I avert my eyes and drape a tablecloth over him before sneaking out the back door.

That means Becca . . .

No!

I run.

When we played together, Gittel and I had made a secret path through the hedges that separated our houses. I follow that path and find Gittel between our two yards, huddled and crying. The men killed her family, too. We make a plan to run into the woods when it gets dark, and follow the stream to the rocky caves where we played last summer. We'll hide there until we figure out what to do next.

We hear a gunshot and know there is no time to waste. We race through the woods to the caves.

For days, Gittel and I hide in the dank caves, making the small parcel of food I brought last as long as possible. When our hunger becomes intolerable, we venture out. I know our path will be dangerous, and I remember my promise to my mother. I can't risk losing her locket, so I hide the coat in the caves. We won't be gone long—we'll get some food and return to our hideout.

Gittel and I stand on the front steps of a farmhouse. I can see fields, and in the distance, woods.

I knock hard on the front door. Nobody answers. I knock again. This time the door opens a crack.

"What do you want?" a golden-haired woman hisses.

"Please help us. We have nowhere to go. We haven't eaten in days," I say.

The woman sighs and opens the door a bit wider, scanning the road and fields. "Hurry." She pulls us inside.

We stand in the middle of a simple room with a plank table to one side and two chairs set up in front of a stone fireplace.

"I'll give you something to eat and a place to sleep for the night, but you'll have to move on tomorrow. My husband will be back, and he is not as sympathetic as I am."

The woman goes to a cupboard and brings out a loaf of bread and a large hunk of cheese. She wraps them in a cloth and motions for us to follow her down the stairs to a small, cold room filled with vegetables and crates. "You can sleep here. If anyone comes looking, hide in one of the crates. Understand?"

Gittel and I divide the bread and cheese, barely taking time to breathe as we shove the food into our mouths. After devouring every crumb, we roll up a few potato sacks and make a bed. Curled up into fetal positions, nose-to-nose, we shiver into slumber.

Sometime during the night, a loud bang startles us from sleep. Half awake, we scramble into an empty crate. I hear deep voices above us, then loud thumps on the steps. Closer, closer, and then someone pulls the lid off the crate and a flashlight shines in my eyes. I scream.

Twisting, kicking, clawing at the hands, I fight with every ounce of strength. Cold metal slams my skull, and everything goes dark.

I am on the floor of Taj's studio, with his black duster draped over my shoulders. "Maggie, come back," he clasps my hands.

Ms. Cherry crouches on the floor next to me, holding a crystal over my head. "That was some story."

"What happened?" I ask.

"You were remembering," Taj says, "out loud again."

Ms. Cherry rocks back on her heels. "This girl you painted. She is more than just a girl. You've tapped into your eternal soul, Maggie," she says. "It's incredible."

Then I remember.

The locket.

CHAPTER TWENTY-FOUR

"The locket! I have to go!"

"Let us know what you find! Taj calls.

I run at full speed, tripping over rocks, winding down the narrow pathways. Hair flying. Feet pounding.

Sucking in breath, I pull open the front door of my house and dash up to my room.

The coat. I feel a bump under the collar and open a seam, working the object toward the opening with my fingers. Finally, a small gold oval slides out, and I gasp.

"It's true," I stammer.

I turn the locket over. The front is decorated in fine filigree. The gold glows softly in the sunlight. I find the release clasp, take a deep breath, and pop it open.

Brown curls, not red.

Dark eyes, not blue.

Is this me from a past life as Freyda?

I examine the photograph to the left. "And if this is me, then this was my mother and my bubbe." I look into the dark eyes of Freyda. "Am I you?"

I might be.

But I'm still not sure.

Reincarnation. Is it really any crazier than believing I was possessed by a ghost?

I type the word into the computer.

My heart pounds in my throat.

CHAPTER TWENTY-FIVE

Ding dong, ding dong, ding dong. The doorbell trills downstairs. Then I hear two sets of feet pounding up the stairs.

"Did you find it, Maggie?" Taj is red-faced, hanging onto the doorway.

Patty is on his heels. "You can't just barge in here!" She turns to me. "If Mom catches a boy up here, we'll be grounded for life."

"Look." I hold up the locket.

"What's that?" Patty asks.

"It was in the coat. I remembered putting it there, before . . ."

"Before?" Patty touches a finger to the gleaming gold.

Taj moves behind me and reads the computer monitor. "You're researching reincarnation?"

I smile. "Yes, and some of it is really convincing."

"So are magicians, Maggie. But we all know magic isn't real," Patty says.

"Take a look at this." I open the locket.

"It's the girl from your painting." Patty reaches out and I drop it into her open palm.

"It was sewn into the seam of the tweed coat's collar." I raise my eyebrow at Taj.

"Just like you said," he exclaims.

"Here's what I found online about reincarnation." I click on one of my bookmarks. But the monitor shifts out of focus. I feel an arm around my shoulders, then nothing.

"I'm going to distract him," I whisper to Gittel. "When I do, run to the river. The dog will lose your scent in the water. Go back to the caves. I'll find you."

Gittel shakes her head, but I know we are only in this situation because of my recklessness. If anyone is to be punished, it should be me.

I twist my body around and clamp my teeth on the guard's wrist. He yelps, letting go of Gittel. His dog locks onto my leg, shaking it back and forth. I bite my tongue so as not to cry out. I don't want Gittel returning to help me. From the corner of my eye I see her disappear into the shadows.

The guard pushes me to the ground. I get up and start to run, but trip over a tree root. Landing hard in a cluster of brambles, the air whooshes from my lungs. I stay perfectly still, catching my breath.

The next thing I see is the orange flare of a gun muzzle. Pain shoots across my chest.

"Judenschwein." He kicks me in the ribs and walks away. "Fuss!" He commands the dog to heel.

The dried grass crunches under their feet as the man and dog leave me to my fate. They seem to have forgotten about Gittel, thank God.

Moments pass. Shakily, I reach up. There is a hole under my left collarbone, and blood pooling under my body. There is a scuffling noise, and suddenly Gittel is by my side, cradling my head in her arms. "Go," I whisper.

"No," Gittel says through quiet sobs.

"I'm dying."

A film clouds my eyes. Behind Gittel I make out the shapes of my mother, father, and sister Rebecca.

My mother kneels by my side, shimmering like stars on a clear, dark night. "Come with us."

"I can't leave Gittel, Mama." I am gasping for breath.

"You can return to her, my bubula." Her voice sings like it is part of the wind. It is in my ear, yet all around me.

I am puzzled. "Return?"

"Yes, in your next life, meina sheyna maydelah. We'll help you find her."

"Gittel," I say in between gasps. "I have to go . . . but I'll come back to you."

"Come back?" Gittle sniffles.

"In my next life. I promise I'll find you." My breath becomes shallower. "I promise, I promise, I promise . . ." I continue to murmur. A bright light appears in the sky and my family walks toward it, beckoning me.

I am lifted out of my bleeding body, a butterfly freeing itself of its cocoon, and I follow my family. The light is so bright I have to close my eyes.

I blink, and the room refocuses. Patty sits on the floor, staring at me oddly. Taj has his arm around me.

"She's back," Taj says.

"Maggie, what were you talking about? Dogs, guns, dying?" Patty's lip trembles.

"I remember being shot under my left collarbone." I say. I pull my collar down to reveal the dime-sized birthmark there.

"What does it mean?" Taj asks.

"They say many people who remember past lives died a violent or sudden death. They often have some type of scarring, birthmark, or even physical deformity related to the tragic event that killed them."

"Incredible," Taj whispers.

There was never a ghost. The coat had triggered my past-life memories. And I remember my promise. *The promise.*

Chapter Twenty-Six

Reincarnation. Taj, Patty, and I huddle around the computer. I click to the page of a reincarnation expert I bookmarked, and read: "Most of my subjects started talking of past-life experiences around the age of three. By the time they reach age five or six, the memories seem to recede until they are practically gone." I spin around in my chair. "But my memories didn't start until I bought the coat. Why not earlier?"

Patty paces the room, avoiding my eyes.

"What's wrong?" I ask.

She bites down on her lower lip and then releases it, leaving two tiny dents. Her mouth opens, then closes as if what she's about to say must be difficult. "Yesterday . . . you . . . said . . . Becca." She pauses between each word.

"Yes."

Tears are in her eyes. "You called *me* Rebecca when we were little. Remember? I showed you the drawing? Well, you also called yourself Freyda."

"I called myself Freyda?"

"You refused to call me Patty." Her voice trembles. "You said my real name was Rebecca and yours was Freyda. You said my nickname was Becca."

"I did?"

"I asked Mom about it, and she had said you were just being silly. But Dad didn't think so. When we were alone he used to ask you all kinds of questions. One day Mom caught him and got really mad. I think it scared her. You know, with everything she went through with Aunt Bridget. She told him to stop with all the mumbo-jumbo.

Don't know why, but when you were around six, you just stopped saying those names—like that article about reincarnation said."

I hold my head in my palms. "I don't remember that."

"It was ages ago; I nearly forgot about it, too. If I hadn't come across that drawing in my box, I might not have remembered. Wait—"

Patty pulls the box out from under her bed. Under old report cards, notes from boys, and pictures of her past movie star crushes, she pulls out the drawing she showed me before, and a piece of manila paper.

"Dad got you to draw pictures of your memories. Mom threw them all away, except these two. I hid them. You drew this for me when you were in kindergarten."

She hands me the crayon drawing on manila paper. It shows two stick-figure girls holding hands, one taller than the other. Both girls have brown hair and brown eyes. Under the tall girl I'd written "FREYDA" in block letters. Under the other girl, I'd written "BECCA." I don't say it out loud, but could Patty have also been my sister in that lifetime?

My excitement starts with a fizz in my toes and bubbles up to my lips. "Do you know what this means? I was a Jewish girl in Auschwitz in my last life, and now, well, now I'm an Irish girl living in the suburbs of New Jersey. I could have been a thousand different people: Muslim, Buddhist, African American, Chinese, who knows, but my soul was always my soul. And if it's true for me, it could be true for everybody."

Even Dad.

Patty lets out a long breath. "Wow, I could have been anybody, too—Marilyn Monroe, Cleopatra—maybe even a boy? Freaky."

"Anybody," Taj says. "Even a weird-dressing Moroccan kid."

"Ouch," Patty says. "All right, I deserved that."

"So now what?" Taj asks.

"Yes, now what?" I whisper back.

A million questions run through my head. How did I live an entire life and never know? Gittel, my best friend, was with me all this time, and I never even realized it? If I hadn't found the tweed coat, would I have ever remembered? Are all people reincarnated? Were Mom and Dad my parents in my last lifetime? Will Dad come back to me one day? And if he does, will I recognize him?

I am Margaret May McConnell, but another me needs to be added to the picture. How will I combine them?

And, do I need to?

Chapter Twenty-Seven

Today is the art show.

Mom tries her hardest to get off from work, but to no avail. Suzi agrees to drive us. She has proven to be a real friend. I should spend more time with her.

Taj meets Patty and me at Silver Lake. Mrs. Valentine calls to say Gittel wants to see me before the show. To my surprise, Gittel is dressed to the nines, her hair done up in a bun and pearl earrings clipped to her earlobes. I'm not completely fooled; I can still see how pale she is under the pink rouge.

"You look great," I say.

"I couldn't look like a *meshugana* at my best friend's art debut," she answers with a smile.

"Mags, go stand next to her and I'll take your picture," Patty says.

I put my arm around Gittel, and Patty captures it with a click of the cell phone. She hands me the phone.

There we are. I don't look to see if my hair is fixed or my smile is good, like I normally would. I don't see a young girl with an old lady, either. All I see are two friends—one whose life is near the end, the other whose life is about to begin.

Mrs. Valentine hovers over her. "Are you sure you feel up to this, Gittel?"

"Never felt better. Now let's get a move on, dears." Gittel taps her foot.

Mrs. Valentine turns to Suzi. "Drive safely. Follow the speed limit. No showing off." She folds a piece of paper in my hand. "Gittel's doctor. Call this number if anything seems off."

"Absolutely," I say.

The five of us pile into Suzi's huge Caddy. Taj, the perfect gentleman, helps Gittel secure her seatbelt.

"Ready?" Suzi yells.

And we are off.

The show is being held in the private home of one of the art school's professors. We coast up a long drive flanked by tall oak trees. Light dances through the curves of the graceful limbs and paints the lawns with shades of green. At the entrance, a valet takes the car and we enter the massive home.

The rooms are filled with gorgeous art on easels and installations of magnificent sculptures. Suddenly, I am not feeling as confident as I was earlier this morning.

Taj hooks his arm through Gittel's and we tour the show. We follow the crowd into the next room.

"Ah, here she is. The artist." Ms. Cherry makes the people clear a path for us. When we reach her, she leans over and whispers, "Your work is generating quite a bit of interest. I've already heard from three people interested in purchasing it."

"Really? You didn't tell them about all the reincarnation business, did you?" If I sell my art, I want it to be on its own merit.

She raises her fingers to her mouth and mimicks locking it with a key. "Not a word. It's a powerful piece on its own."

That's when I see Gittel making her way toward the easel. Tears stream down her face. I walk up beside her and squeeze her hand.

She squeezes back and whispers, "Our souls will always be free."

CHAPTER TWENTY-EIGHT

The following week a letter arrives in the mail. It is very thin. Is that a good thing or a bad thing?

Don't be disappointed, I tell myself. There is always next year.

I begin reading.

Dear Ms. Margaret McConnell,

It is with great pleasure that we would like to grant you a full scholarship to the Peabody Academy.

I flop down on the sofa. I kept my promise to my dad. I'll be attending the Peabody Academy.

"I did it, Dad!"

I hop on my bike and pedal toward Silver Lake. I can't wait to see Gittel again, my friend of at least two, maybe more, lives.

When I arrive, Mrs. Valentine meets me at the door. "Oh, Maggie, I'm so glad you're here. Miss Berk's been asking for you."

"Great. I want to see her, too." I head for the steps.

"Wait, I need to talk to you."

I follow Mrs. Valentine into the parlor and sit down.

"Miss Berk is very sick, Maggie. She made me promise to keep it a secret but—" She dabs her eyes with the corner of a crumpled tissue. "She's been in and out of consciousness all night. The doctor is with her now. She doesn't have long. I think she's holding on to see you one last time. You brought her a lot of happiness, dear."

"No!" She can't leave me yet. I've just found her!

I hurry up the stairs and run down the hall. My sneakers squeak on the wood floors as I skid to a stop in front of Gittel's room.

A man with a stethoscope gives me a grim look. "Freyda?"

"No, I mean yes. I'm Freyda." The words feel funny, yet familiar, in my mouth.

The doctor pats my shoulder and leaves the room, shutting the door softly behind him.

Through blurry eyes I see Gittel in her bed. She is pale as ice. I take her hand; it's warm, and I don't want that warmth to leave me.

"Freyda, you're here." The corners of her mouth turn up; her eyes are bright but unfocused.

"Yes, Gittel." My voice hitches. "I'm here."

"I see them." She smiles. "Momma, Papa. Even Minka, that silly kitten." Her thin hand reaches out.

I glance around the room and see nothing. But I know what it means; her time with me is quickly fading. I want to chase them away, tell them it isn't fair.

"I'll be back, Freyda. I'll find you just like you found me," she says, her voice thin as autumn leaves. "I promise."

I hug her tightly, trying to keep her in my world, but the soft breath that was blowing gently against my neck ceases, and I know she's gone.

After a few moments I let her go, tears streaming down my face. "Goodbye, Gittel," I whisper, "don't forget your promise."

I already miss Gittel more than I ever could have imagined. There was so much we wanted to talk about, but I know one day we'll be together again.

At home, I hang my tweed coat in the closet, taking one more sniff of Chanel Number Five, the scent of my mother from another lifetime. At first, after I found out about my past, the scent made me sad, but now it gives me comfort. My last mother's body has been dead for decades, but she is in the universe somewhere, either back on Earth or waiting for the right time to return. I know our goodbye was not final. One day, somehow, we'll meet again.

I now know that Dad isn't lost to me forever, either. And Aunt Bridget isn't lost to Mom forever. There's no such thing as goodbye.

I slide the black dress I wore to Dad's funeral from its hanger. Think I'll donate it to the thrift shop. I smile and close my closet door.